"You make it a habit to propose to strangers?"

"Not generally. But I'll make an exception in your case."

Lyla shook her head. "Men like you don't even ask out women like me."

Wyatt frowned. "Men like me and women like you?"

"Hot guys who know they're hot," she clarified. "Don't you dare say you don't know you're hot. And I'm the opposite of hot."

"Oh, you're hot, all right."

And he so wished he hadn't blurted that out. He knew how to keep things close to the vest, and he darn sure shouldn't be saying something like that to Lyla. Especially since it was the truth.

WANTED

—

USA TODAY Bestselling Author
DELORES FOSSEN

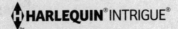
HARLEQUIN® INTRIGUE®

Recycling programs
for this product may
not exist in your area.

ISBN-13: 978-0-373-69734-2

WANTED

Copyright © 2014 by Delores Fossen

Printed in U.S.A.

ABOUT THE AUTHOR

Imagine a family tree that includes Texas cowboys, Choctaw and Cherokee Indians, a Louisiana pirate and a Scottish rebel who battled side by side with William Wallace. With ancestors like that, it's easy to understand why *USA TODAY* bestselling author and former air force captain Delores Fossen feels as if she were genetically predisposed to writing romances. Along the way to fulfilling her DNA destiny, Delores married an air force top gun who just happens to be of Viking descent. With all those romantic bases covered, she doesn't have to look too far for inspiration.

Books by Delores Fossen

CAST OF CHARACTERS

Marshal Wyatt McCabe—Raised at the notorious Rocky Creek orphanage, he's a widower still nursing old wounds when he uncovers a plot to use his late wife's embryo to force him to tamper with a murder investigation.

Lyla Pearson—The assistant director of the CSI unit that's processing the evidence from an old murder at Rocky Creek. But Lyla has no idea that her job and desire for a baby has put her on a collision course with Wyatt and with danger.

Kirby Granger—Sixteen years ago, this now retired marshal rescued Wyatt and five other boys from the Rocky Creek orphanage, but he might have cut corners to do that.

Stella Doyle—Kirby's longtime friend. She, too, worked at Rocky Creek and might know more about the present danger than she's willing to admit.

Travis Weston—A wealthy rancher with shady ties to Rocky Creek.

Sheriff Zeke Mercer—He was friends with the notorious Rocky Creek headmaster, whose murder is now being investigated.

Greg Hester—Zeke's business partner, but he has secrets that could give clues about the killer.

Billy Webb—It was his father who was killed sixteen years ago, and while Billy claims he's innocent, he had a huge motive for wanting his father dead.

Chapter One

Marshal Wyatt McCabe adjusted his binoculars and studied the woman. Lyla Pearson. She was leading a roan mare into the barn just behind her small ranch house, and from what he could tell, she appeared to be talking to the horse. Maybe even singing to it.

She sure didn't look like someone on the verge of committing a felony.

Not yet anyway.

One thing was for certain—he'd never met her. If he had, Wyatt was pretty sure he would have remembered her even though there was nothing much about her that stood out.

Five foot seven or eight. Average build. Brown hair that she'd gathered into a ponytail.

She was wearing no-frills jeans and a weathered buckskin coat—practically a uniform for someone working with horses. Something he knew a little about, since he worked his own family's ranch.

Wyatt checked his watch. A little past seven in the morning, which meant Ms. Pearson would soon change her cowgirl *uniform* for her job as assistant director of the San Antonio Crime Scene Unit. He had every intention of following her there, too. In fact, he didn't intend to let her out of his sight until he figured out what the heck was going on.

He *would* get answers.

And those answers extended to the baby she was carrying.

There was no baby bump that he could see. Probably too early in the pregnancy for it, but Wyatt wasn't a baby expert. However, from everything he'd read about her, Lyla had wanted a baby for years even though she was single and not in a relationship.

What Wyatt needed to know was why she'd wanted *this* particular baby.

She disappeared into the barn, probably to stable the mare, and when she came out, she stopped and looked around as if she sensed someone was watching her. Wyatt ducked lower behind the pile of boulders, though he figured he was hidden well enough. He'd had a lot of experience doing surveillance duty in rural settings during his six and a half years as a marshal.

The sharp January wind slapped at her, and it was cold enough that when her breath mixed with the chilly air, it created a split-second foggy haze around her face.

Still, she didn't move.

She continued to glance around.

Even though she wasn't a cop, she had cop's eyes. Maybe a cop's instincts, too, which Wyatt hoped didn't kick in. He needed to figure out what she was up to before she even realized he was on her trail.

Finally, she moved, walking toward her house, and Wyatt was so caught up in watching her that he nearly missed the movement on the back side of the barn. It was just a blur of motion. Maybe a horse. But with everything else going on, that seemed too much to hope.

Wyatt volleyed glances between her and the barn,

and he saw it again. This time, he got more than a blurry glimpse. No horse. It was a man, and he was lurking behind the barn. Wyatt watched, wondering if Lyla knew about her visitor. Maybe he was even her partner in crime.

But the man didn't call out to her.

And she didn't seem to notice him.

Hell.

This was not a complication he needed right now.

If the guy wasn't her partner, then Wyatt needed to know why he was there. Because he figured someone skulking around a barn didn't have the best of intentions. Unless he was a lawman, that is.

Wyatt took a harder look. The guy was dressed in camouflage clothing. There was no sign of a lawman's badge, so Wyatt drew his Colt from his shoulder holster and eased onto the top of the boulders. Wyatt started hurrying toward Lyla. Anything he did right now was risky, but the risk went up a significant notch when he saw the man dart from the barn to the back of her house.

The guy was armed.

Lyla didn't appear to be.

And worse, she was smack-dab out in the open. If this wasn't her partner, then why was he there, and did that gun mean he was going to try to kill her? Maybe this was someone opposed to what Lyla had already set into motion, and if the man killed her, Wyatt would never know the full truth.

Plus, there were other reasons to keep her alive, and the biggest reason of all was that baby she was carrying.

"Get down!" Wyatt shouted to her.

She whirled around as Wyatt had expected her to do. And froze again. The gunman darn sure didn't freeze. He darted out from the barn and took aim.

At Wyatt.

Wyatt dropped to the icy ground. "I'm Marshal Wyatt McCabe," he shouted.

The guy ducked back behind the barn, but Wyatt didn't see or hear anything to indicate he was on the run. Too bad, because if there was a gunfight, then Lyla could be caught in the cross fire. Definitely not something he wanted.

Even worse, Wyatt couldn't call for backup. He'd checked his phone shortly after he'd parked his truck on the hidden curve of the road—not far away at all—and the whole area was a dead zone. No reception whatsoever.

"Get down!" Wyatt called out to her again.

Thankfully, this time she got moving and did as he'd ordered. Lyla landed on the dead winter grass, yards from her front porch and the safety of her house. There was nothing she could use to hide behind or for protection, and that meant Wyatt had to get to her, fast.

He levered himself up but kept as low as he could. He also kept his Colt aimed and ready. And he started running. He braced himself to dive back to the ground if necessary, but when the gunman peered out from the barn, he didn't fire.

"Drop the gun!" Wyatt ordered.

He was close enough to Lyla now that he heard her make a sound of surprise mixed with a whole lot of fear. Her reaction made Wyatt think she hadn't known that an armed man was less than thirty feet away from her.

An armed man who clearly wasn't listening to a thing Wyatt was telling him to do.

The guy didn't drop his gun. He stayed put, just tossing out the occasional glances. Once Wyatt had Lyla safely inside, he was going to do something about this nonlistening moron. That didn't mean killing him. No. That was the last thing Wyatt wanted, because he wanted answers from him, too.

"Don't move," Wyatt reminded Lyla when she lifted her head. She dropped back down but looked at him as if trying to figure out who he was.

Or rather, *pretending* to do that.

Since her pretense and the reaction to the gunman could all be a ruse, Wyatt kept his attention on both her and the gunman. He made his way across the narrow dirt road that stopped directly in front of her house. Each step was a victory because there were no shots being fired at them. He really wanted to keep it that way.

Wyatt hurried the last few yards to her, and he moved directly in front of her, making sure he was between her and the gunman.

"What's going on?" she asked, her voice shaking as hard as the rest of her.

"I was hoping you could tell me." He took aim at the barn and stood. "Is your front door locked?"

"No."

Good. Though he'd figured she hadn't bothered to lock it. Not usually much crime out in the rural part of the county. Of course, *usually* wasn't the norm right now.

"Stay behind me," Wyatt instructed. "We're going inside."

Where he hoped she wouldn't try to kill him. But then, he figured her plan didn't include murdering him.

Nope.

She or someone else had put too much in motion to outright kill him.

Well, unless the plan had changed and someone was trying to cut their losses and make sure there were no loose ends with equally loose lips. If that was the case, then both Lyla and he could be targeted to die.

She didn't argue about going inside with him, and Lyla slid her hands over her stomach and practically pressed herself against his back as they inched across the yard. Wyatt could feel the tight muscles in her arms. Could feel her warm breath hit against his neck.

And he could feel her fear.

He shifted his position a little as they went up the steps. He had to keep Lyla shielded, but he also had to make sure the gunman didn't try to go in through the back of her house.

That led him to his next problem.

If someone was trying to nix a plan that was already in motion—like this one—there might be another attacker waiting inside. Or maybe this was all part of Lyla's plan—get him inside so she could move on to the next step.

Whatever the heck that was.

Despite the *don't be stupid* warning echoing through his head, Wyatt opened the door and stepped inside, keeping her next to him. His attention and gun slashed from one side of the living room to the other.

Nothing.

Well, nothing that he could immediately see anyway. It wasn't a large room, but there was a dark red sofa and two chairs. Not easy hiding places, but he checked anyway. Then he checked for what could pose the most immediate danger.

Lyla Pearson herself.

"Are you armed?" he asked, but didn't wait for her to answer. Wyatt shoved his hand inside her coat and gave her a quick pat down.

She gasped and tried to push him away, but Wyatt held his ground. "I don't carry a gun," she insisted.

"Maybe not, but you have one registered to you."

Her eyes widened. "How'd you know that?"

Wyatt just tapped the marshal's badge clipped to his belt.

Lyla still looked confused by all of this. Heck, maybe she was. After all, if she'd truly set up the gunman pretense, she would've had to have known that Wyatt would be there at that exact moment. He'd kept this visit secret. Not even his five foster brothers knew, and they were all marshals, too. He hadn't wanted to tell them anything until he'd figured out what was going on.

The figuring out started *now*.

"Back door locked?" he asked. He pulled her inside, keeping her against the jamb.

"I'm not sure."

"Stay put," Wyatt snarled, and he hurried into the kitchen. If anyone was hiding, they would have to be in the fridge, because the pantry door was wide-open and he could see inside. He turned the dead bolt on the door to lock it.

She didn't ask why he'd done that, but he could feel her fear go up a notch. Or maybe she was faking that, too. At any rate, she was breathing through her mouth, and the pulse on her throat was skittering a mile a minute.

Wyatt went back to her, waited. Listened. But he didn't hear anyone inside, or out, for that matter. So, he grabbed the cordless landline phone and handed it to her. "Call 9-1-1 and request backup."

Her hand brushed against his when she took the phone, and for just a split second, their eyes met. Hers were brown, just as her file had said, but what wasn't in her file was they were deep and warm.

Oh, man.

He didn't need to be thinking of her eyes. Or anything else, for that matter. She could be one of the most conniving criminals he'd ever met.

Or maybe an innocent pawn.

Until Wyatt knew which, her eyes and the rest of her were off-limits.

While she made the call, Wyatt got her all the way inside and kicked the door shut. He locked it. But he didn't move. He stayed put, waiting to make sure they were indeed alone. Waiting, too, to see if she'd make some kind of move.

She didn't. Lyla called 9-1-1 just as he'd asked.

The window on the east side of the room was both a blessing and a curse. It allowed Wyatt a decent view of the back side of the barn. The last place he'd spotted the guy with the gun. But that window was also a danger, since the gunman could see them and shoot right through the glass.

"A deputy's on the way," Lyla relayed once she'd finished the call.

Good. But the nearest town, Bulverde, was a good thirty minutes away, and he was on his own until then.

"Who's out there?" she asked.

"You don't know?"

Her breath rattled in her throat. "I have no idea." She shook her head and caught onto the door, maybe because she didn't look too steady on her feet. "He can't shoot me. I'm pregnant and he could hurt the baby."

If this was an act, she was damn convincing.

Wyatt glanced around, looking for the safest way to approach this—for both him and her. "Get down on the floor in front of the sofa."

It wasn't a perfect location. Not by a long shot. But it

would get her out of direct line of fire of that window, and with her on the floor, she wouldn't be able to attack him.

She moved to do just that but then stopped and stared at him. "What's going on?"

He didn't have to lie about this. "You're going to tell me that after I take care of the guy by the barn."

Her stare tightened into a glare, and with that glare aimed at him, she eased down onto the floor.

That freed him up to hurry to the hall entry, where he spotted three doors. Probably two bedrooms and a bath. All the doors were open, but unlike with the pantry, he didn't have a clear look inside any of them.

"Why are you here?" she asked. "How did you know there'd be a gunman at my house?"

Tricky questions, both of them. If she didn't truly know the answers, then they were both in some Texas-sized trouble.

"I'm involved in an investigation, and you might have something to do with it," he settled for saying.

"I don't understand. What investigation?"

Wyatt knew he couldn't dodge her questions for long, but he really had to make sure another gunman wasn't inside the house. "Don't get up," he warned her, and he hurried into the hall for a quick check of the bedrooms and bath.

"What investigation?" Lyla repeated.

Even though he'd stepped into her bedroom, Wyatt had no trouble hearing her. "Jonah Webb's murder."

She mumbled something he didn't catch, but Wyatt ignored her, had a look under the bed and in the closet. Everything was neat and in its place. Definitely no smoking-gun evidence that he could use to arrest her on the spot.

When he was satisfied they were alone and there was

nothing immediate for him to find, he hurried back to the living room and met Lyla's glare. It was worse than the other one she'd aimed at him.

"Jonah Webb," she repeated. "He was the man from the orphanage who was murdered years ago."

Sixteen and a half, to be exact.

She studied his face. Then his badge. "You're one of the marshals who were raised at the orphanage." Again, he couldn't be sure if her surprised tone was fake or not.

"Rocky Creek Children's Facility," he supplied.

He tried not to go back to those bitter memories. Failed. Always failed. But bad memories weren't going to stop him from doing his job. Wyatt went back to the center of the living room so he could keep watch to see what the bozo with the gun was going to do.

"Webb's body was found, what, about six months ago?" she asked.

"Eight. The Rangers are still investigating it." He paused, to try to figure out if this was old news to her, but he couldn't tell. "Webb's wife, Sarah, confessed to the murder, but she had an accomplice. Unfortunately, she wasn't able to say who her accomplice was, because she's in a coma."

And Sarah had been that way since she'd tried to kill his brother Dallas and Dallas's wife, Joelle. Dallas had had to shoot the woman, and she'd been in a coma ever since.

"Your foster father is a suspect," Lyla whispered. "I remember reading that in one of the reports."

Yeah. Kirby Granger was indeed that. And worse, he might have actually done it, though Wyatt never intended to admit that aloud.

Not to her.

Not to anyone.

Especially if it turned out that Lyla Pearson was living proof that Kirby was not just innocent but that someone else was willing to do pretty much anything to cover their own guilt.

"You're a suspect, too," Lyla added. Her breathing kicked up a notch, and she got to a crouching position. Maybe because she was just now realizing she could be in danger—from him. Heck, she might even be thinking of running.

Wyatt nodded, watching both her and the window.

She blinked, and he saw the doubt in her eyes. Lyla shifted her position again. Oh, yeah. Definitely planning to run.

"I'm not sure what's going on," he said. "But I suspect you know a lot more than you're saying."

The remark had no sooner left his mouth when Lyla leaped to her feet and started toward the hall. Probably to get the .38 that was somewhere in her bedroom. Wyatt hadn't seen the gun, but he figured it must be in the house.

Wyatt latched on to her, trying to stay gentle, but it was hard to do when she brought up her knee to ram into his groin. He had no choice but to drag her to the sofa and pin her body with his.

It didn't put him in the best of positions. He could no longer see the window or the gunman, but it stopped her from getting away.

Lyla frantically shook her head and tried to punch him. "Why are you doing this?"

He dodged her fist, barely. "Why are *you* doing this?" And Wyatt dropped his gaze to her stomach.

"I don't understand." The words rushed out with her breath.

Maybe she did. Maybe she didn't. But Wyatt decided

to test a theory or two. "I think you got pregnant so you could manipulate this investigation."

She stared at him as if he'd lost his mind. "My baby has nothing to do with Jonah Webb's murder."

"You sure about that?" he countered.

"Positive," Lyla mumbled, but there it was. The doubt that slid through those intense brown eyes. "Why would it? Why would my baby have anything to do with this?"

Wyatt took a deep breath. Had to. "Because that baby is mine."

Chapter Two

Lyla figured either Marshal Wyatt McCabe was insane, or someone had told him some huge lies. Either way, she had to get away from him.

She put her hands against his chest and gave him a hard shove. She might as well have been shoving a brick wall, because he didn't budge. He wasn't exactly what she would call muscle-bound, but he was solid.

"Please." Lyla tried to reason with him. "Let me go. Neither me nor my baby has anything to do with you or the murder investigation."

The marshal made a *yeah right* sound, but he did move off her. Not far, though. He levered himself up but continued to loom over her. Continued to volley glances out the window, too. Did that mean the man with the gun wasn't working with Marshal McCabe?

Lyla wasn't sure.

She wasn't sure of anything any longer except that she wanted to get away from both men. Her keys were already in her car, which was parked in the garage. If she could get to it, she might be able to escape.

Might.

But she couldn't risk getting shot. Of course, these men might have something much worse in mind than just hurting her. They might want to kill her.

But why?

She shook her head. Marshal McCabe obviously wasn't the only one with questions.

"Who's the gunman?" she asked him again. Maybe now that the facade of the helpful lawman was gone, she'd get some straight answers, because the ones she'd gotten from him so far hadn't made a lick of sense.

McCabe lifted his shoulder. "I don't know. Your bodyguard maybe?"

"I don't need a bodyguard." But she rethought that. "At least, I didn't until twenty minutes ago. Clearly, I need one now to protect me from you."

He studied her as if trying to decide if that was a lie or not. It wasn't. In fact, everything she'd told the lawman had been the truth, but he obviously didn't believe her.

Lyla tried to remember everything she knew about Marshal McCabe, but other than the sketchy details about the Webb murder investigation, she drew a blank.

"We've met before?" she asked, though she was certain they hadn't. McCabe was the sort of man a woman tended to remember. Tall, good-looking. Dark brown hair and gunmetal-blue eyes.

Yes, definitely the sort to be remembered.

"No," he answered. "But you know me."

"I don't," she insisted.

That baby is mine, he'd said, but he had to be wrong about that.

Well, maybe.

"I used in vitro fertilization to get pregnant," she explained, though judging from the flat look he gave her, he already knew.

"Yeah. At the Hanover Fertility Clinic in San Antonio," he supplied. "You had the procedure done two and half months ago, on your thirty-first birthday, and it worked on the first try. You got the news two weeks later that you were going to be a mom."

A chill went through her. It was downright creepy that this stranger knew such private things about her, but it chilled her even more to know he might have told the truth about the baby being his.

"The clinic assured me that the donor I used would be anonymous," Lyla explained. "In fact, I insisted on it, because I intend to raise this baby myself."

"Yeah," the marshal repeated. "Old baggage. I know about that, too."

Lyla snapped back her shoulders, ready to blast him for invading her life and privacy this way. It wasn't any of his business about her failed relationships.

She had to get her teeth unclenched so she could speak. "I want you to get out of here now. The deputy's already on the way, and if you don't leave, I'll have him arrest you. I don't care if you're a marshal or not."

"Oh, I'm a marshal, all right, and I believe you manipulated that in vitro procedure so you could force me to cooperate."

Lyla tried to throw her hands in the air, but McCabe pinned them to the sofa. "And how could I possibly have manipulated it?"

He glared at her. "By switching mine and my late wife's embryo with the one you should have received."

Oh, yes. He was crazy.

"I didn't switch anything. There was a slim-to-none chance that I'd get pregnant the old-fashioned way, because my body rarely produces eggs, even with fertility treatments. So, I used the donation the clinic gave me." She paused just long enough to gather her breath. "And what possible proof do you have that it was yours?"

"All the proof I need." But McCabe paused, mumbled

some really bad profanity. "Four months ago I hired a surrogate to have a baby, using the embryo that my late wife and I'd stored at a clinic. Not Hanover," he quickly added. "Another one in San Antonio. But then the surrogate changed her mind and decided not to go through with the pregnancy."

Lyla mentally went through all that. "And you think I somehow got yours and your wife's embryo instead of the anonymous one I requested."

"I know you did," he fired back. "Last month, the clinic called me and said the embryo was missing. They said maybe it'd been stolen or accidentally donated, and I followed a very hard-to-follow paper trail that eventually led to you."

Oh, mercy. Maybe it was true, then, but Lyla wasn't just going to take this man's word for it. "I want to see this paper trail."

Marshal McCabe tipped his head toward the barn. "After I hear what your gun-toting friend has to say."

"He's not my friend!" she practically shouted. "And so what if the clinic accidentally gave me your embryo? It doesn't matter. I don't want you in my life, and I don't want you part of my baby's life."

Except there was the possibility about this being his late wife's embryo. No. Did that mean he'd have some kind of legal claim?

That couldn't happen.

"The switch wasn't an *accident*," he insisted. But then he shook his head. "At least I don't think it was. I think there's something bad going on here and that you're a key player in this wrongdoing."

Lyla couldn't argue with the *something bad* theory. He was there, right in her face. But she'd done nothing wrong and had taken no shortcuts in getting pregnant with this baby.

"I don't know where you got your information about me, but there's no reason whatsoever that I'd want to have your baby." And she didn't bother to say it nicely, either. "I want you arrested and out of here. That'll happen as soon as the deputy arrives."

Soon couldn't be soon enough, though. Lyla prayed that whoever the sheriff had sent out was speeding to her ranch right now.

"If I explain to the deputy what I've learned, maybe he'll arrest you," McCabe threatened right back. "Because one way or another, you will tell me what's going on."

"I have no idea," Lyla insisted, but she was talking to the air, because the marshal's attention was fastened to the barn now. He practically jumped to his feet and snapped in that direction.

Alarmed at the concern that she saw in his eyes, Lyla jumped up, as well, and followed his gaze. There wasn't one man but two out there now. Both wearing camouflage fatigues. Both armed.

Oh, God.

Now she had three armed men on her ranch.

"Either your second bodyguard just showed up, or you've done something to piss off someone other than me," McCabe growled.

Even though she didn't trust the marshal, that didn't mean Lyla could ignore what he'd just said. Maybe she had riled someone. After all, she was the second in charge of a huge crime-scene-unit lab, and processed all kinds of evidence.

"You think those men are here to hurt me?" she asked, peering out at them.

"Hard to say."

She was tired of the vague answers. "Then guess," Lyla demanded. She pinned her attention to the gunmen, too. If they moved one inch, she'd have to move as well. She prayed they didn't start shooting into the house.

McCabe shook his head. "Maybe there's someone who doesn't want you involved in this."

Well, she certainly fell into that category. Lyla didn't want to be involved even if she had no idea what *this* was. Still, that was something she would have to work out later. After she had some way to protect herself.

Lyla moved, ready to race toward her bedroom to get the .38 she had in the back of her nightstand drawer.

"I don't think so," McCabe snarled.

He hooked his left arm around her waist, dragged her to him and anchored her against his body. She'd only known him a matter of minutes, and it was the third time he'd put his hands on her. Lyla wanted to do something about that.

Actually, she wanted to punch him and run.

But she couldn't risk hurting the baby. No. As angry and scared as she was, her best bet was to wait for the deputy and maybe try to reason with this man, who claimed to be the father of her child.

A father who might be a criminal.

Lyla tried to think back through their entire conversation. Not easy to do, with her heart and mind racing and with McCabe plastered against her. It was hard to think or breathe with him so close. Still, she forced herself to do just that, and she went back to the part of their conversation before he'd dropped the embryo bombshell.

"Why did you think I had anything to do with the Webb murder investigation?" she asked. Lyla also kept watch on the two gunmen.

"You don't…yet," McCabe said.

Despite the clear danger outside, that caused her attention to snap to the marshal. "What do you mean?"

"I mean you'll be put in charge of compiling the final investigation, the one that'll determine who's responsible for Jonah Webb's murder."

Lyla was shaking her head before he even finished. "Not possible. The Texas Rangers have their own crime lab, one of the best in the country."

"And soon the governor will say there's a conflict of interest, that the head of the Ranger lab once worked on a case with one of their prime suspects, Kirby Granger."

"Your foster father," she mumbled. "It's true?"

McCabe nodded. "True that they worked together. Not true about the conflict of interest."

That probably wouldn't matter. Appearance was everything in this sort of investigation. The sixteen-and-a-half-year-old murder had drawn national attention, and the governor and the Rangers would want to make sure the right people were held responsible for the crime.

Still, there was something about this that didn't make sense.

"Even if the governor transferred the investigation to the San Antonio Crime Scene Unit, they wouldn't put me in charge of the case. He'd choose my boss, Dean Mobley."

"Your boss will excuse himself and insist that you take over," McCabe said without hesitation or doubt.

Not likely. Mobley and she didn't see eye-to-eye on much. "Why would he do that, huh?"

"I don't know, but he will."

Lyla huffed. "He won't." And she would have added more to that argument if she hadn't heard a welcome sound.

A police siren.

Thank God. The deputy was nearly there. And she hoped he had plenty of backup.

McCabe cursed again, and for a moment she thought it was because of the siren. Maybe it partly was. But he didn't even spare the front of the house a glance, despite the fact that the police cruiser would soon arrive there. He still had his attention on the two men by the barn.

"Stay inside," McCabe ordered, and he started for the back door.

Lyla didn't intend to let him leave. She wanted him arrested. She reached to latch on to his arm, but then she saw the movement.

The two gunmen.

They were no longer behind the barn. They were running. Getting away.

McCabe threw off her grip, and with his gun aimed and ready, he hurried to the back door. Lyla followed him, but there was no way she could stop him. Not with that rock-hard strength.

He'd barely made it to the door before one of the men stopped. Pivoted.

And fired.

Chapter Three

The sound of the bullet blasted through the house.

"Get down!" Wyatt shouted to Lyla.

Wyatt got down, too, but he stayed near the back door so he could keep an eye on the gunmen. One was already racing across the pasture, away from the house, and the other didn't even take aim before he fired another shot and then took off running, as well.

Hell.

Wyatt couldn't let them get away, but he also couldn't risk one or both circling back around and coming after Lyla. He had no idea if she was innocent or not, but by damn, he was not going to let her get gunned down.

"What's happening?" Lyla asked. She was on the floor, thank God, one hand over her head and the other over her stomach. He hoped she stayed that way, though her hands would be a paltry shield for bullets.

"Someone's trying to kill me," Wyatt relayed to her. "Or maybe you."

But there was something off about this attack, if it was indeed a murder attempt. For one thing, the men had waited way too long before shooting. In the twenty minutes or so that Lyla and he had been in the house, two gunmen could have torn the place apart with a shower of bullets.

Maybe that meant they'd wanted her alive.

Or scared.

If so, they'd succeeded in doing both. Lyla was trembling on the living room floor, but she hadn't been hurt, and that meant the baby was safe.

Wyatt tried not to think about that. Tried not to think about the deception that had gone into creating this child. He just focused on the job, and right now the job was keeping Lyla and the baby safe and stopping those gunmen.

The moment that Wyatt heard the cop car brake to a stop in front of the house, he bolted out the back door. Not because he was afraid of being arrested. No, he could handle that. But now that Lyla had someone else to protect her, it was time to see what he could do about the gunmen.

Wyatt had to go after them.

Both of the men were running, their backs to Wyatt. He considered shooting but dismissed it. If he hit one, the other could return fire, and he was still too close to the house to risk that.

Wyatt leaped off the porch and hit the ground running. Not the easiest thing to do in cowboy boots and winter gear, but the men were weighed down by equipment belts, which no doubt held extra ammo. Maybe extra weapons, too. They'd obviously come prepared for an attack that they'd barely carried out.

The pasture wasn't that deep, unfortunately, and behind it was a fence and then a heavily treed area. He wanted to stop the men before they could disappear into those woods, but they had too much of a head start on him. When Wyatt saw the first man reach the fence, he knew he had to do something.

"Stop or I'll shoot," Wyatt called out.

Still not listening, they didn't stop. Both of them continued to run, and the one in the lead latched on to the top rung of the wood fence and started to hoist himself to the other side.

Wyatt fired at him.

The shot was off because he hadn't stopped and aimed, but it got their attention. The guy on the fence turned and fired right back. Wyatt saw the bullet slam into the ground and kick up dirt. Much better than it going toward the house.

Wyatt fired another shot. Ducked. But the one on the fence didn't take the bait this time. He scrambled over the top and disappeared into the trees.

Wyatt turned to fire at the other one, but the shots began to blast through the air. Obviously, the gunman on the other side of the fence hadn't run away and left his partner after all. He was trying to save his sorry butt, and to save his own butt, Wyatt had no choice but to dart behind an old cast-iron bathtub that'd been turned into a watering trough.

He cursed, waiting, but knowing this would allow the second man to get away. Wyatt lost count of the number of shots fired, all of them smacking into the trough and the ground around him.

But they stopped just as quickly as they'd started.

Wyatt waited another second or two and then took off running again.

Neither man was in sight now, and since he didn't know the area, Wyatt couldn't even predict which direction they'd gone. Maybe he would be able to find their footprints and follow them.

"Stop!" someone yelled from behind him. Not Lyla. A man, probably the deputy.

Wyatt spared him a glance over his shoulder. Yep, a

deputy in uniform, all right, and he was standing with his gun drawn on the back porch. It was a risk, because the lawman might shoot him in the back, but Wyatt was so close to the fence now that he took his chances. He barreled over it and dropped to the ground.

There were footprints. Plenty of them, and some had bits of dried leaves and twigs in them, which could mean they were several days old. Later, he'd need to ask Lyla about who had access to this part of the property, but he was betting these weren't the footprints of a neighbor.

Someone had been watching her for a long time.

He lifted his head and listened for any sound of footsteps. Nothing. Just the wind. But he soon heard something he didn't want to hear.

An engine starting up.

Wyatt raced toward the sound, weaving his way through the trees and scraggly underbrush, and it didn't take him long to get to a clearing with a trail. He caught just a glimpse of the black SUV as it disappeared out of sight. He didn't even have a chance to get the license number.

Oh, man. He didn't need this.

Without thinking, he yanked out his phone, and he got a quick reminder of why he hadn't already called one of his brothers. Still no service out in this rural area. That meant he needed to get to a landline ASAP.

He also needed to face that gun-pointing deputy.

Wyatt meandered his way back to the fence and was about to climb over it when he spotted something.

A camera mounted on one of the trees.

He followed the angle of the lens—it was aimed directly at Lyla's house. Yeah, someone had been watching her.

But who?

Wyatt figured the camera might give him some clues about that, so he ripped it from the tree and climbed back over the fence. The deputy was still on the porch, but there was no sign of Lyla, who was hopefully still inside and on the floor. That was because the gunmen might make a return visit and this time launch another attack.

"Marshal McCabe," the deputy said as Wyatt got closer. He was a pencil-thin man with pink flushed cheeks and nearly white blond hair. "I'm Deputy Walter O'Neal."

"I hope you called for backup, because the shooters got away in a black SUV. They used what appears to be an old ranch road."

The deputy nodded. "Got two other deputies on the way. You can give us a description at the sheriff's office, 'cause I need to take you in for questioning."

Yeah, Wyatt had figured that, and he had no plans to resist. Or even argue. The sooner he finished his business with the deputy, the sooner he could have the camera analyzed and figure out the identities of those gunmen.

"Lyla said you accused her of some wrongdoing," O'Neal added when Wyatt made it to the porch.

"I did." He held up the camera. "And this might prove it." However, it was more likely to prove her innocence, since she had no reason to put her own house under surveillance, unless it was part of some security system to make sure no one got too close.

Like him.

"I did nothing wrong," he heard Lyla repeat, and she stepped onto the back porch to join them. But not for long.

Wyatt took her arm and put her right back inside. "She shouldn't be out in the open, because of the gunmen."

And he turned to the deputy. "You need to bring her to the sheriff's office with us."

"She insisted on coming," the deputy said, sounding a little uncertain about that. Or maybe his uncertainty was just for Wyatt and the shots that'd been fired. "Though I did suggest she see a doctor while I deal with getting your statement."

"The men really got away?" she asked, her eyes wide. Lyla grabbed her coat and purse from the peg next to the door that led to the garage.

Wyatt nodded and held up the camera. "Any idea who's been watching you?"

That didn't help ease the look of concern on her face. "No."

He hadn't expected any other answer from her, but then she stopped. "Three days ago someone from the electric company showed up and said he needed to do some repairs on the lines. He seemed, well, a little suspicious. Like he was nervous or something."

That was a start. "I'll make some calls and see if he was legit or not. Also, if there's a surveillance disk in here, we might get a better look of the gunmen's faces." Of course, there probably wouldn't be a disk. It likely had some kind of wireless feed to another device.

One that the gunmen had almost certainly taken.

Wyatt doubted they were so incompetent that they would have left something like that behind. Still, he might get lucky. He would have a closer look later.

"I take it all of this is part of some official investigation?" O'Neal asked.

"An investigation, yes," Wyatt answered. "Official, no. Not yet anyway. I'm here for personal reasons."

He waited to see if Lyla had told the deputy about the in vitro switch, but she didn't say a word. Wyatt figured that would change, though, when they got to the sheriff's office. Lyla was a crime scene analyst, bound by the law, and she no doubt trusted this deputy more than she trusted him.

Yeah, she'd tell, all right.

"I'll let you keep your gun," O'Neal said, leading them out the front and to his patrol car. "For now."

Wyatt didn't like the guy's attitude, but he had to admit it was a generous concession. If their situations had been reversed, Wyatt wouldn't have let him stay armed.

Since there was a bulky equipment bag in the front passenger seat, Lyla and Wyatt got into the back. She didn't say a word to him, but she did shoot him another glare. Wyatt gave her one right back. So far, the evidence was pointing to the fact that she might be a pawn, but until Wyatt knew for sure, he intended to be as wary of her as she was of him.

"What will happen now?" she asked, directed not at Wyatt but rather the deputy.

"We'll start with your statements," he answered, his attention shifting all around. Wyatt was doing the same thing, looking for those gunmen. "I guess neither of you recognized those two men?"

"No," Wyatt and she answered in unison. That seemed to annoy her, too. "But the marshal probably thinks I'm lying about that."

"The marshal figures she's telling the truth," Wyatt countered. "About that anyway." He looked at her for the rest of the explanation. "Those bullets were real, and I don't believe you'd put the baby at risk by hiring idiot gunmen to shoot at or near you."

"I wouldn't." Her chin came up. Her voice was strong. "This baby is my life, and…" She snapped away from him.

Wyatt could finish that for her. *This baby is my life, and you have nothing to do with it.*

Or something along those lines.

She'd already said she didn't want a baby daddy. Wyatt had to make sure that was the truth. Then he'd figure out what to do with that truth and everything else that seemed to be hitting him at once.

"Call ahead," Wyatt instructed the deputy, "and arrange for Lyla to be checked out by a doctor. Just in case."

He expected her to argue with that, too, and maybe it was on her mind when she opened her mouth. But then she just slid her hand over her stomach.

"Thanks," she said under her breath, and the deputy made the call.

While he did that, Wyatt checked his own phone. He finally had service, so he made a call and asked one of his foster brothers, Marshal Declan O'Malley, to find out if the utility company had sent someone to Lyla's house. With one thing down, he mentally went through the long list of other calls he had to make.

But the ringing of Lyla's phone stopped him.

"Mr. Mobley," she greeted the caller. Her boss. "I might not be in this morning. I'm on my way to the Bulverde sheriff's office....Oh, you heard about the shooting." She paused. "No, I'm fine."

Lyla opened her mouth to say more, but Wyatt heard the chatter on the other end of the line. He couldn't tell what her boss was saying, but it had captured her complete attention.

"What?" she finally said, quickly followed by "Why?"

More chatter, and Wyatt still couldn't make out enough of it to tell what was going on, but he hoped like the devil it wasn't more bad news. He'd had enough of that already.

"We'll talk when I get to the office," Lyla snapped, and she ended the call. It took several moments, though, for her to look at Wyatt. "Mobley excused himself from the Jonah Webb investigation, and the Rangers want me to take over."

Not exactly a surprise. "I hate to say I told you so, but I did."

"It could mean nothing," she concluded, but the worry in her voice said it was a whole lot of something. "Mobley got another job. A civilian company with much higher pay. They want him to work with a legal watchdog group that's retesting evidence from old criminal cases."

"The timing's suspicious, but it gives me another lead. The person who offered Mobley the new job could be behind the rest of this."

She swiveled around to face him. "What exactly is the *rest of this?*" She glanced uneasily at the deputy and moved closer to Wyatt. "If this is some kind of plan to get me to falsify evidence, it won't work," she whispered.

"It might be that." But he just didn't know.

"The in vitro could have been just an honest mistake," she whispered a moment later. "Mobley's new job could be a coincidence."

"And the gunmen? The camera?" Wyatt pressed. "More coincidences? Because when there are that many of them, we call that a pattern."

He almost told her about the information trail that had led him to her, but his phone buzzed. Declan.

"First of all, the utility company didn't send someone to Lyla Pearson's house," Declan said the second Wyatt answered. "And second, what the hell's going on?"

Considering that Wyatt had been about to ask his brother the same thing, this wasn't a good start to what he needed to be a good conversation. "Are you referring to something specific? Because there's a lot going on."

"The Rangers got an anonymous tip that you're trying to influence the Webb murder investigation."

Ah, man. He didn't need this. "No, someone else is trying to influence it." And maybe already had. "Look, this is too complicated to get into over the phone—"

"Does it have anything to do with Lyla Pearson, the assistant director of the San Antonio CSU?"

That sent an uneasy feeling knifing through him. "It does. Why? Other than the fact that she didn't get a real service call from the electric company, what do you know about her?"

"According to the criminal informant I just talked to, she's in big trouble, Wyatt, and you should avoid her at all costs."

"Too late."

Declan cursed. "You're with her?"

"Yeah. Now why don't you tell me why that's a bad idea?" Wyatt insisted.

"Because according to the informant, by going to her, you just signed her death warrant."

Chapter Four

Death warrant.

Those two words kept going through her head, and each time, they robbed Lyla of her breath. Not that her breath was anywhere near steady yet, despite the several hours they'd spent at the sheriff's office and hospital getting her checkup. All was well with the baby, thank goodness, but it might be a while before she could rein in this feeling of panic. Her racing heartbeat, too. And the adrenaline crash.

Yes, she had that going on, as well.

Despite the clean bill of health from her obstetrician, none of this stress could be good for the baby. But then, neither were those bullets.

It was the too-fresh memory of those bullets and those two words, *death warrant,* that had made Lyla get in the truck with Wyatt after they'd finished giving their statements to the deputy.

Now she was debating that decision to allow him to place her in his protective custody. She wasn't thinking straight, but what she did know was that Wyatt seemed to want to keep her alive and safe. And he seemed capable of doing that.

Capable of wrecking her life, too.

But maybe once she got all of this sorted out, there'd

be no need for protection. No need to dodge gunmen lurking on her ranch.

"You're sure this criminal informant was telling the truth about the death threat?" she asked. "Because if he's a criminal, how can you trust him?"

"He's getting paid to spill his guts, and if what he spills is a lie, then the payments dry up." He paused, mumbled some profanity. "Unfortunately, this guy's reliable, and he said somebody's got their eye on you."

"But he didn't know who." It wasn't a question. Lyla had already pressed Wyatt on that when he'd first told her about the threat. "Then how could the criminal informant know anything about the other details if he doesn't even know the person's identity?"

"Bad people talk. Sometimes too much, and this guy plays a fly on the wall so he can make money. He says someone's going to force you to cooperate with altering evidence, and if it doesn't work out, then you'll be eliminated. *Dead*," he clarified.

Even if the informant had lied, she wasn't immune to just the threat of it. Mercy, how had things gotten this far out of control?

"I should be in San Antonio P.D.'s protective custody," she tossed out there. "Not yours."

He spared her a glance with those intense blue eyes but kept his attention on the rural road that would take them to his family's ranch.

Which she was certain wasn't a good idea at all.

"Those guys took shots at me, and that makes this federal now."

It was weird. Though he'd practically barked that at her, his voice was far from a bark. Everything that came out of Marshal McCabe's mouth seemed smooth as silk.

And genuine. Yes, he was a charmer, all right. Even when he was accusing her of assorted crimes.

Like stealing the embryo that belonged to him and his late wife.

"You can't possibly want me at your family's home," she reminded him.

"I don't. But I don't want you dead, either. And right now, I'm your best shot at not being dead."

Even that came out as an easy drawl, but it still slammed into her. She couldn't die. Couldn't be shot. Because anything that happened to her, happened to her precious baby, as well. But somehow, someway, she had to distance herself from this silver-tongued cowboy lawman. Once she was at the ranch, she'd need to start making calls to arrange for some private security. And a bodyguard or two.

"I'm sorry, by the way," he added a moment later. "If I hadn't uncovered what was going on, the person behind this wouldn't have ordered a hit on you. At least not until you'd done everything they want you to do."

None of that was reassuring, especially the last part. "But what do they want me to do?"

"I don't know yet. But it won't be legal, and doing it won't necessarily keep you alive. Right now, I'm your best shot for staying in one piece."

Again, not reassuring, since it was obvious he distrusted her. Probably hated her, too, because he still had his doubts about her involvement in all of this. She wasn't sure if she even wanted to address that or just make those calls to get her out of there.

Wyatt took the turn toward the ranch, and moments later the house came into view. Except, *house* didn't seem the right word to describe something that size. She'd heard of Kirby Granger's spread, of course, but she hadn't expected this. Miles and miles of pastures. Hundreds of Angus cows. And she spotted four barns, along with a small house and another massive brick one that looked as if it'd recently been built. Yet another one was under construction.

Heaven knew how many people and buildings were on the parts of the property she couldn't see.

Wyatt pulled to a stop directly in front of the main house, where there were several ranch hands milling around, all armed. A middle-aged woman with graying red hair stepped out.

"Declan called," she greeted them, the worry obvious in her voice. "He said someone shot at you."

But Wyatt just shrugged. Like his voice, it seemed to be an easy drawl, too. There was certainly no crazy panic in his body language, but Lyla was sure there was plenty in hers.

"The others call Wyatt a bullet magnet," the woman added, glancing at Lyla.

Lyla's gaze whipped to him. "Why do they call you that?"

Wyatt frowned. "Why do you think?"

"Oh, God," she mumbled.

"God's probably the only one who hasn't taken a shot at me yet."

The woman gave him a scolding look. "His brothers say he's a bullet magnet because someone's always trying to mess up his pretty face. But they don't say that around me. They know I don't like joking about stuff like that."

She came closer when Lyla and Wyatt made it onto the porch, and she slipped her arm around Lyla's waist. "I'm Stella Doyle, a friend of the family. I take care of Wyatt and the others when they let me."

"The others?" Lyla asked.

"Wyatt's foster brothers. Dallas, Clayton, Harlan and Slade. Mine and Kirby's own son, too—Declan. They're all marshals like Wyatt here, and they're all my boys."

Wyatt brushed a kiss on the woman's cheek. "Where's everyone?"

"Dallas took the womenfolk and Clayton's baby to his and Joelle's place." She tipped her head in the direction of the new house, which Lyla had noticed. "He said he talked to you about that."

"He did. I just thought it'd be better if there were fewer people here tonight. Is Harlan with them?"

Stella nodded. "Slade, too. You're expecting some kind of trouble?"

"Trying to prevent it." Wyatt glanced at the curvy dark-haired woman who was sweeping the porch. A maid, no doubt. "When'd you hire her?" he asked Stella.

"Last week. Why?"

"I just want the ranch on lockdown for a while. Give her and any other new help a few paid days off. That includes ranch hands."

Stella gave an uneasy nod, and she wasn't the only one who was uneasy. It hit Lyla then. If someone had been watching her, then maybe they'd done the same to Wyatt. With all the activity going on, it would be easy to get someone onto a ranch this size.

"And now I need help with our guest," Wyatt continued. "This is Lyla Pearson, and she'll be staying with us for a while."

Stella volleyed glances at both of them. "Your girl?" she asked Wyatt.

"Yes," Wyatt said at the exact moment that Lyla blurted out, "No."

Lyla was about to ask why he'd told such a lie, but

Wyatt just shot an uneasy look at the woman sweeping, took Lyla by the arm and got her inside.

"Later," he added to her in a whisper when Lyla opened her mouth to ask about that whopper. He looked at Stella again. "I need a couple of the ranch hands to go out to Lyla's place and take care of her horses."

"I can do that myself," she insisted.

"Those gunmen might return." And that was all he had to say to put her heart in her throat. She loved her little house. The only home she'd ever had, and now she couldn't go back.

Maybe ever.

It might never feel safe there.

"Her address is in the glove compartment of my truck," Wyatt explained to Stella. "But tell the ranch hands to go there armed. Just in case."

Stella's eyes widened a little, but Lyla didn't think it was so much from surprise as from fear or dread. Heaven knew how many incidents like this the woman had gone through, living with six active marshals and a retired one.

"Come on," Wyatt told her. And it took Lyla a moment to realize he'd shifted the conversation to her. "You're staying with me until further notice."

Wyatt didn't give her time to disagree with that order. With his grip still firm on her arm, he ambled them through the maze of halls and to a home office. His, judging from the way he ushered her inside, closed the door and eased down in the seat behind the desk.

"Right about now, you're thinking of running," he said, and he proceeded to go through some emails on his laptop. "But you can't."

Lyla huffed. She was tired of this knight-in-shining-Stetson routine, especially since Wyatt didn't seem the knight type. More like a pirate. A hot one.

Something she wished she hadn't noticed.

Hard not to, though, with those rock-star looks and that devil-may-care attitude. This was exactly the kind of man she avoided.

But was attracted to anyway.

Lyla shoved that attraction aside, put her hands on his desk and leaned in to get right in his face. "I want answers, and I want them now."

He held up his finger in a *wait a second* gesture and finished reading the email. "All my brothers are tied up with this shooting and the investigation. My brother Declan sent the camera to the crime lab," he said when he finished reading whatever was on the screen. "I was right about it not having a memory card, but we might get some prints or trace. Plus, Declan might be able to track down who bought it. It's not something available at the corner store."

Good. That was a start, to find out who was behind this, but Wyatt went on to the next email, ignoring the fact that she was right in his face and wanting an explanation about his *yes* answer to Stella about her being his girl.

And why he believed she was carrying his child.

"My other brother Clayton is looking into who just hired Dean Mobley for his new civilian job with the watchdog group," Wyatt went on. "But his new employer is actually a dummy corporation. A good front, though, and it won't be hard to break through the layers, especially since it was probably set up just to hire him. It'll disappear as soon as they're finished with Mobley and you."

She thought about that a moment. "How'd you know my boss would be offered this new job?"

"Criminal informant. The same one who said I'd signed your death warrant."

The new info whirled through her head like a tornado, and even though Lyla wanted to appear strong and resolute, she wasn't. To make matters worse, she had a sudden dizzy spell and would have sagged to the floor if Wyatt hadn't caught her.

But he didn't just catch her.

He scooped her up in his arms and deposited her on the leather sofa positioned in front of a massive wall of books.

"You need me to call a doctor?" he asked, going to the small fridge in the corner. He brought her back a bottle of water, and he opened it for her. The man certainly knew how to take control.

Something she had to put a stop to.

"No doctor. I just get dizzy sometimes."

She wouldn't mention the occasional morning sickness and these strange hormonal changes in her body. Sometimes she felt like crying her eyes out, and other times she felt like a randy teenager.

Heck, she hadn't been a randy teenager even when she was in her teens.

Her body was playing one of those stupid hormone tricks on her now. Probably because Wyatt was there, just inches away, with his drop-dead-hot face looking down at her.

Like her earlier thoughts, she pushed that hormone surge aside, too.

She had help with that. Also practically right in her face was the photo on the end table. A beautiful woman in a wedding dress. Smiling from ear to ear, and her dreamy smile was directed to her equally dreamy husband.

Wyatt.

"My wife," he explained, following her gaze. "Ann passed away two years ago from a rare blood disorder."

"I'm sorry," Lyla said, because she didn't know what else to say. Words wouldn't help the hurt that she still heard in his voice. But since he'd brought up his wife, it was time to start addressing the thousand-pound gorilla in the room.

"Why do you think I got your embryo?" she asked.

He did another of those effortless shrugs. "It went missing, and the theft was well hidden. The clinic didn't discover it until last month. Since then, I've tried to locate every woman in the state who used a donor embryo to get pregnant. Only twenty-three."

"That you know of," she argued. "Maybe some clinics keep that private, since the law requires it."

He gave her a flat look. "I am the law, and I was looking for something that belonged to me."

Yes, and he'd obviously been tenacious. "There's no proof I'm carrying your baby."

"You're the only one who makes sense. There was the wife of a high-level D.A. looking for a donor embryo, but the Webb investigation couldn't have been shifted to him. You're the only one who could affect the outcome of this case."

She shook her head. "That still doesn't prove it."

"No, but a test would, and we're lucky that you've already had an amnio."

Lyla flinched. "How'd you know that?"

Another flat look. "I had someone look into your medical records."

"You hacked them."

"Yeah," he readily admitted, and he wasn't apologizing for it. "You had one done three weeks ago to rule out a uterine infection. You didn't have an infection, but at your request the doctor didn't provide you with other info."

"I didn't want to know if it was a boy or girl."

"That's fine. That's not important anyway, but what is important is that test would have given me confirmation that you're carrying my child."

It would. And that suddenly terrified her. If this was his baby, there was no chance this man would just back away. "I can call the doctor and ask for the results." Even though that was the last thing she wanted to do.

She really had to get out of there, and she reached in her purse for her phone.

Wyatt stopped her again. "Your test results were stolen."

Lyla looked up at him, blinked. "Wh-what?"

"Stolen," he repeated. "The doctor hasn't told you yet because I'm not sure he knows. The results went missing from the lab, but there's another sample of the amniotic fluid. The thief didn't manage to get that, because it was stored at a different location in case the doctor wanted it retested."

Oh, God. All of this had gone on, and she hadn't even known about it.

"I'm having that second sample of amniotic fluid tested," Wyatt explained. But he wasn't so calm and cool right now. A muscle flickered in his jaw. "And I should have the results in a day or two."

"*I* should be the one to get those results," she challenged.

But that was as far as her challenge got, because his phone rang. Maybe because he thought she might bolt, Wyatt kept his eyes on her while he took the call.

"Declan," he greeted, and even though she couldn't hear what his brother was saying, it caused his forehead to bunch up. "I'm putting you on speaker so Lyla can hear this."

Please, not another death threat or news of some other violation to her privacy that she was just being informed about.

A moment later, his brother's voice began to pour through the room. "As I said, the lab lifted a print off the camera, and we got a match. Nicky Garnett. He's got a record a mile long."

Lyla shook her head. The name meant nothing to her. "You know him?"

"We know him," Declan confirmed. "He works muscle for a rich rancher, Travis Weston. No record for him, but that doesn't mean he shouldn't have one. The man's dirty and with plenty of money to cover his dirty tracks."

Another head shake. "What does this Travis Weston have to do with me?" she asked.

Declan didn't jump to answer that time. "I'll let Wyatt finish the explanation, and I'll get started on bringing Travis in for a little chat."

"Do that," Wyatt agreed, and he ended the call and looked at her. "Travis and Jonah Webb were old friends."

Oh, she didn't like the direction this was going. She'd just been put in charge of the evidence gathered from Webb's murder, and now his old friend had ties to a man who'd not only spied on her but had fired shots at Wyatt?

"Webb used to send some of the boys from Rocky Creek to work on Travis's ranch," Wyatt continued. "Including me. At best the arrangement was shady, probably illegal, and there were rumors that Travis used some of the boys to move illegal weapons in and out of Mexico."

She pulled in her breath. "He used you for that?"

Wyatt shook his head. "Probably because Kirby was looking out for me. Kirby was a marshal at the time. A good one. And they wouldn't have wanted him to have an insider like me in on their schemes."

Lyla tried to make sense of all of this, but she couldn't. "So, maybe Travis wants to make sure I help prosecute his friend's killer? Maybe he doesn't want me dead after all."

Wyatt made a soft grunt. "Webb and Travis had a falling-out. No one's sure about what exactly, but they were bitter enemies before Webb was killed." He paused. "Travis is a suspect in his murder, and the Rangers have been questioning him along with keeping any evidence they might have against him close to the vest. I'm sure Travis would like nothing more than the head CSI to clear him of any possible charges."

She swallowed hard. Lyla had thought it would help if she had a name to go with this mess, but from the sound of it, that wasn't a name she wanted associated with her.

"Travis is a killer?" she risked asking.

"Oh, yeah. If he hasn't killed already, it's only because he hasn't had to. He usually hires muscle like Nicky Garnett to kill for him."

It felt as if a chunk of ice had settled in her stomach, and Lyla pressed her fingertips to her mouth to try to steady the trembling. "How do we get out of this?"

"For starters, we lie. And not some little white lies, either. Big ones. We turn this con right on them and eliminate their reason for wanting you involved in any of this. That'll keep you and the baby safe."

Maybe it was the dizziness, but Lyla wasn't following him. "How do I do that?"

Wyatt stooped down, going onto one knee so they were literally eye to eye. "You'll marry me—*today*."

Chapter Five

Wyatt had expected Lyla to be shocked. And to argue, of course. But what he hadn't expected was to see the color drain from her face.

Clamping her hand over her mouth, she motioned toward the side door. "Is that a bathroom?" she asked.

He nodded, got up and opened it for her before Lyla ran inside. And she did run, fast, kicking the door shut behind her just seconds before he heard her throw up.

Wyatt wasn't sure if that was a major insult or if it was part of the pregnancy. Either way, it was a reaction he hadn't counted on. He needed her tough, asking all the questions that needed to be asked so they could move on to the next step in what he hoped wasn't a stupid plan.

Too bad it was the only plan he had.

"You okay?" he asked.

"Morning sickness." And he heard the toilet flush before she turned on the water in the sink. She splashed water for what seemed an eternity before she finally came back out. She was drying her face with a hand towel.

"You've lost your mind," she said, brushing past him and heading back for the sofa. She gulped down some of the bottled water.

"Wouldn't be the first time."

Her left eyebrow came up. "You make it a habit of proposing to strangers?"

"Not generally. But I'll make an exception in your case."

A burst of air left her mouth. A laugh, but not from humor. She shook her head, pushed away the strands of hair that'd slipped onto her face. "Men like you don't even ask out women like me. So, needless to say, your proposal is more than a shock."

Wyatt frowned. "Men like *me* and women like *you?*"

She made a sound to indicate the answer was obvious. It wasn't. Of course, maybe he'd missed something.

"Men like you," she repeated, waving her hand over his face. Then his body. She stopped waving when she got to his zipper area, probably because now that she was sitting down, it was sort of in her face.

He stepped back.

"Hot guys who know they're hot don't ask out bookworm tomboys like me," she clarified.

Wyatt was flattered. Then riled.

Then confused.

"Don't you dare say you don't know you're hot," she added.

He had to shrug. Yeah, women seemed to find him attractive. The wrong women anyway. The only one he'd had any luck with was Ann, and the luck hadn't lasted long. They'd had only three years of marriage before she'd passed away.

Lyla waved her hand over her own face. "And I know I'm the opposite of hot."

"Oh, you're hot, all right."

And he so wished he hadn't blurted that out.

He wasn't a blurter. Or someone who used the word *hot* to describe a woman. He knew how to keep feelings under wraps, and he darn sure shouldn't be saying something like that to Lyla. Especially since it was the truth. They had enough to work through without adding "hot" labels to each other.

Oh, man.

She glanced at his zipper again. And that stupid, brainless part of him decided it was time to give him a reminder that'd it had been way too long since he'd had a woman in his bed.

Well, he wasn't getting this woman there.

Except the plan was for him to do just that. He wouldn't be in his bed with her, of course. And that was no clearer than it was right now with them staring at each other and with the heat rising in the otherwise cool room.

"I think it's time for a change of subject," Lyla said, holding the damp towel against her throat.

Wyatt couldn't agree more, and it wasn't as if they didn't have a whole boatload they had to discuss.

"I've done some damage control," Wyatt started. "There are no official records around to prove you received a donor embryo."

Her eyes narrowed a bit. "Do I want to know how you discovered that?"

"No." And he waited to see if she'd challenge it. She didn't, so he continued. "Of course, whoever's behind this knows, because that's the person who likely set it all up. Unless you did it."

She huffed. "Why would I do that? I don't even know you, and I don't have a personal stake in this investigation. Well, I didn't until the shooting this morning."

Oh, yeah. It was personal now. "The only reason I could come up with was because you might be working with the person who wants the evidence altered."

Her eyes narrowed. "I don't break the law."

Admirable, but as Kirby always said—never mistake the law for justice. Over the past couple of days, Wyatt had done a lot of law *bending,* but he'd done it to make sure justice was served.

"So you're not in on the plan," Wyatt concluded, taking her glare as proof of her innocence. Besides, she didn't feel guilty, and while a gut feeling didn't sound good in a report, Wyatt always trusted his gut. "It means soon someone will contact you about what you're supposed to do."

"And according to you, they'll kill me if I don't cooperate. Then they'll kill me once they're finished with me."

Wyatt didn't have any doubts about that. "It's why we need a fake relationship. And a legal marriage. I already have the license." Best not to tell her how he'd come by that, but it'd required some string pulling, too.

"A license already?" she challenged. "But why? You thought I was guilty before you showed up at my place. Heck, you still don't trust me."

"I can't let my trust issues keep you in the path of a killer. And you're right—when I came to your place, I didn't know if this was your plan or not. I don't think it is," he quickly added when her eyes narrowed, this time to slits.

"How generous of you. Yet the point is, you didn't trust me, but you got the license."

"Just in case. I was trying to plan for any contingency." Because the stakes here were sky-high. "And I have a justice of the peace waiting for my call. As soon as you say yes, he'll be out here to marry us. Once we have this dirtbag behind bars, then we can get a quick annulment."

She looked at him as if he'd grown an extra nose. "How will saying *I do* possibly stop this?"

"Being married to me will exclude you from taking over the evidence in the investigation."

Ah. She got it. The light went through her eyes. Followed by some expected darkness. "Because you're a suspect in Webb's murder."

"My whole family, including a couple of sisters-in-law, are all suspects. No way would the governor allow you to stay on the case if you're my wife. And if we can convince everyone that we made that baby the old-fashioned way."

She glanced at his zipper again. "No one will believe we're lovers."

He had to disagree. "They will if we're married. Maybe not so much if we just lie and say we're together. That'd be a little harder to pull off, but marriage should convince even the person behind this."

"How?" she repeated.

"By planting so-called proof of our secret affair. Hotel receipts, doctored photos. Remember that trip you took to Dallas last month?"

She nodded. Then frowned. Probably because he'd invaded her privacy again. Of course, he'd invaded it so many other times that she should be getting used to it by now.

"Well, I can come up with a witness who'll verify we were in Dallas together." She opened her mouth to object, but Wyatt moved on to the next point. "You didn't tell anyone at work about the donor embryo."

"No." She pulled in a long breath. "I'd planned to tell them once I started showing."

"Then lucky for us you're not showing. Right now, the only people who know are us, your doctor—and he's agreed to keep it quiet—and the person who orchestrated all of this."

She stayed quiet a moment. "And for him or her to dispute what we're saying, they'll have to come out in the open."

Bingo.

Well, the person could just try to kill them because he or she was now riled that their plan hadn't worked, but Wyatt kept that to himself. Lyla had enough to deal with already. And besides, a marriage would give him a good reason to keep her right by his side so he could protect her.

The problem would be first and foremost the danger. It might not immediately go away. The next problem was this blasted heat. Lyla darn sure didn't look like a tomboy bookworm, and an unwanted attraction created a distraction that could get them killed.

"If this person only wanted my cooperation with the evidence in the investigation, then why try to kill me?" she asked.

"I don't think it was a planned attempt to kill you. The guy was probably supposed to keep an eye on you, to make sure you didn't try to talk to me or any of the other suspects who could be burned by falsifying evidence. Then, when I showed up, he panicked and started firing."

Lyla stared at him. "What stops them from *panicking* again?"

"Me." Yeah, it sounded cocky, but he would do whatever it took to keep her safe.

She groaned, wiped her face again. "You can't possibly want to go through with this marriage."

"I don't. But it'll cover several hot spots. Other than saving you and the baby, you can't be compelled to testify against me."

That got her attention. "Testify against you? For what?"

"For all the corners I cut while trying to figure out what's going on. Corners I'm cutting now to protect you."

With that tossed out there, Wyatt waited for the rest of her argument. And there would be more. From everything he'd learned about her, Lyla was a cautious woman, and she wouldn't just jump into this.

And that meant he had to push.

"You're doing this for the baby," she said. It wasn't a question.

"The baby's a big reason. I want him or her safe. For that to happen, I have to keep you safe, too."

Ah, her eyes narrowed again. "Even if I have no intentions of sharing this baby with you."

"Even then." Though he'd have something to say about that sharing if the amnio results proved he was indeed the father. If he was, he'd challenge her for full custody.

And he'd win.

No way would he let someone else raise his and Ann's child. But that wasn't the reason he wanted this marriage. He had to put an end to the danger.

"There isn't much time," he pressed. "The sooner we get out the word that we're married, the sooner you'll be pulled from the case and the sooner this bozo will back off."

She didn't jump to agree. In fact, she didn't jump to do anything, but he could see reality creeping into her eyes.

"Is there another way?" she asked.

"I haven't been able to come up with one." And he'd tried hard. Despite his player reputation, he didn't take marriage vows lightly.

"We could pretend to get married," Lyla suggested.

"I considered it, but it doesn't take care of your testimony against me. Besides, if the governor finds out it's fake, you could be charged with obstruction of justice."

She groaned, but he talked right over the sound. "There's also the concern that the person behind this could use a fake marriage to manipulate you."

And that wasn't exactly a long shot.

After all, the person had manipulated this pregnancy and had spent some big bucks to put all of this in place with Lyla's boss's new job, the surveillance and the gunmen. The only way to neutralize all of that was to take Lyla completely off the playing field. The culprit had to believe not only that she was involved with Wyatt, but that she was committed to him.

"You have to think of the baby," he reminded her.

"I know!" she practically shouted. That seemed to sap the rest of her energy, and she looked up at him.

On the verge of saying yes. Wyatt was sure of it.

But his phone buzzed. Wyatt looked at the screen to see if he could let it go to voice mail, but the name that popped up had him doing a double take.

"Billy Webb," he mumbled.

Lyla looked as confused as he was by this call. "Connected to Jonah Webb?"

"His son. And another suspect." Well, in some people's eyes. Billy's dad had been an abusive jerk when he'd been the headmaster at the Rocky Creek Children's Facility. Webb had beaten Billy enough times that if he'd retaliated against his father, Wyatt wouldn't have exactly called it murder.

More like doing the world a favor.

Still, they were back to that justice-and-the-law conflict, and in the eyes of the law, Billy was a suspect. One who happened to be calling Wyatt.

"Marshal McCabe," he answered. Best to keep this

professional. And quick. He still had some convincing
to do in the marriage department.

"I tried Dallas first, but he was out of cell phone range,
so I decided to call you. I'm out at the Rocky Creek facility going through some of my mother's things."

Because his mother lived in the cottage on the facility grounds. Well, she had before she'd gone into a coma
after being shot.

Wyatt froze.

"Did your mother come out of the coma?" he asked.
That was the only reason he could think of that Billy
would be calling him.

"No, but she's improving. She's even opened her eyes
a couple of times and said something to me."

"What'd she say?" Wyatt demanded.

"Just gibberish. Something about a tape, but I don't
remember her mentioning anything about a tape before
she went into a coma."

"Could she have recorded something? Like maybe a
conversation?"

"Maybe. But if she did, the tape's not at her cottage.
I looked right after she mentioned it but didn't find anything. I finally gave up the search and figured I could
ask her once she wakes up for good. The doctors don't
think it'll be long before that happens."

Wyatt didn't know whether to be happy about that or
not. Sarah could clear him and everyone in his family.

Or she could name one of them as her accomplice.

Even worse, it was possible she had a taped conversation to prove it. Of course, the woman might be talking
out of her head. After all, her injuries had put her in a
coma. Injuries she'd gotten while trying to cover up the
fact she'd murdered her husband.

"I didn't call about my mother," Billy went on. "I

thought you should get out here and see what's going on. There's a new team of CSIs out here, and one of them found something."

Though he wasn't sure he wanted Lyla to hear this, she apparently did. She got up and came closer. Very close. And that was when Wyatt hit the speaker button.

"They found old blood spatter on the wall in one of the rooms. Not my dad's office. But in Stella's quarters."

Hell, that was not what he wanted to hear. Stella was like a mother to him. But yeah, she had motive. Because she'd lived and worked at the children's facility when a lot of the abuse was going on. Along with Sarah's help, Stella could have indeed killed Jonah Webb.

"Describe the spatter," Lyla said, and she didn't sound scared anymore. She sounded like the CSI that she was.

"Who is that?" Billy demanded.

"A close friend," Wyatt lied. "We can trust her."

He hoped.

Billy hesitated, and for a moment Wyatt didn't think he'd add more. Finally, he cleared his throat. "Someone had painted over the spatter, but they saw it with some kind of special light."

"A UV light," Lyla provided.

"You should get out here," Billy insisted. "Because I'm thinking they'll try to use this to arrest Stella." And with that, Billy hung up.

Wyatt stared at the phone and tried to work through what Billy had just told him. There wasn't much to work through, though. He needed to know exactly what'd been found in that building.

He grabbed his keys from his pocket and then looked at Lyla. It was risky, leaving her, but he didn't want to pull his brothers away from what they were doing.

"You can stay with Dallas and the others at his house,"

he let her know. It wouldn't be comfortable. Sort of a baptism by family fire. "But don't talk about the baby or the proposal. I need to tell them in my own way."

A way he hadn't quite figured out yet.

"I want to go with you," she insisted. "I want to get a look at that spatter. It happens to be my area of expertise, and I can help you determine what happened. Or if it's been staged. Considering everything else that's going on, someone could have planted the blood there."

He was shaking his head before she finished. "This isn't your fight."

"To heck it's not. Someone's trying to kill me because of this *fight*. I'm not asking your permission. I want to see that crime scene, even if I have to hire a bodyguard or two to go with me."

Wyatt jammed his thumb against his chest. "I'm your bodyguard. And there's that little thing about conflict of interest."

"I'll be an observer. I won't touch the evidence or even talk to the investigators. But I want to see what they've found. And if it's legitimate, I want to stop anyone from tampering with it."

It was a good argument, but he had a better one. "Until we're married, you're in danger. I don't want you out there."

She looked at the marriage license. Then at him. "You're sure that's the only way to keep me and the baby safe?"

"Yes." And Wyatt prayed that was true. If this gamble failed, the consequences could be fatal.

Lyla pulled in a long breath. And nodded. "All right. Let me get a look at that blood, and then…" She stopped, gathered more breath, as if she might choke on the words. "I'll marry you."

Chapter Six

Lyla's heart dropped when she heard what Wyatt said to the person he'd just called. Justice of the Peace Elliot Stowe.

"Meet us at the Rocky Creek Children's Facility," he told the man. "I have the bride and license. You can marry us at the end of the road that leads to the facility. We'll be there in twenty minutes."

"We're doing this now?" she asked the moment Wyatt ended the call.

Wyatt didn't take his eyes off the road or their surroundings. As he'd done since their quick departure, his gaze kept darting to the side and rearview mirrors of the SUV he'd taken from the ranch.

"I'm not taking you inside Rocky Creek until we're married," he insisted. "It's the only way to ensure your safety."

"But there are CSIs and probably cops out in the building. You'll be there, too. Heck, it's probably one of the safest places in Texas right now."

He looked at her, those sizzling eyes showing some anger. "You agreed to this."

"Yes, but I thought I'd have some time to adjust."

And change her mind along with coming up with a different plan.

Mercy, this was happening too fast. She needed some downtime so she could think. But then Lyla remembered the sound of those bullets tearing into her place. Any one of them could have hit Wyatt, her or the baby, and she couldn't risk that again.

"Swear to me there's no other way," she said.

But he didn't swear. Well, he swore some profanity, but he didn't give her a charming or terrifying spin on why this had to happen. Right now, she needed some logic to hang on to.

"Consider this," he finally answered. "I think you're carrying the baby that I've wanted for the past five years. Heck, all of my life. I'll do whatever it takes to protect you. That includes putting my life on the line to save you."

Oh.

Well, that was something to hang on to, all right. Heaven help her, she believed him. About that part anyway.

"Swear on your wife's grave that this isn't an attempt to get custody of this baby when he or she is born."

No profanity this time. No quick answer, either. And that didn't do anything to steady her nerves.

Lyla groaned.

"I won't use the marriage to try for custody," he finally said, "and that's the only promise I can make."

She studied his expression, especially his eyes. Well, as much of them as she could see, considering he was still doing lookout. Lyla groaned again when she realized this argument was over. Both the physical one and the one inside her.

She was going to marry Wyatt McCabe.

A man she hardly knew.

She hoped this wasn't the worst mistake of her life.

She'd made some doozies in the past, but this could top them all.

But it could also save her baby.

Right now, that seemed the only thing that really mattered. That, and putting an end to the danger. Things couldn't continue this way, because the stress could cause her to miscarry.

That thought crushed her heart.

She'd planned and waited so long for this baby, and here someone might snatch it away from her.

Lyla spent the rest of the drive nibbling on her bottom lip and trying to work through the panic she was starting to feel again. How could her life have changed so much in just a few hours? And it might continue to change, for the worse, if they couldn't put a stop to this nameless, faceless person who'd want to manipulate her by using an unborn child.

Wyatt took the turn to the Rocky Creek facility, but there was a car on the road between them and the building. He reached for his gun, causing her heart to thud against her ribs, but he reholstered when the ginger-haired man and elderly woman stepped from the vehicle.

"Slide over toward me," Wyatt instructed her. "That's Elliot Stowe and his secretary, Adele Bedford."

"How did they get out here so fast?" Lyla thought she'd have a least a few more minutes.

"Stowe's a justice of the peace in the town just a few miles from here. He brought his secretary because we need a witness."

Wyatt had thought of everything, but when their gazes met, Lyla could have sworn she saw some uncertainty there. It vanished, however, when the JP and his secretary got into the backseat of the SUV. Because Lyla still hadn't moved yet, Wyatt unhooked her seat belt and slid her closer. Until she was tucked into the crook of his arm.

"Make it fast," Wyatt told the man.

Lyla doubted Stowe could do anything slowly. His muscles were tight and wired. Ditto for his expression. His Adam's apple was bobbing. Clearly he wasn't comfortable with this, either. However, his secretary just seemed puzzled about the whole ordeal.

Wyatt handed the man the license, and without even making introductions, Stowe started the vows. "Do you, Lyla Marie Pearson, take this man, Wyatt David Mc-Cabe..."

Lyla heard the words, saw them form on the man's mouth, but she was still dealing with the shock when it came time for her to say *I do.* Wyatt gave her a nudge on the arm, and she mumbled the words that she prayed she wouldn't regret.

"I do."

A few moments later, Wyatt repeated the words. And Stowe pronounced them husband and wife. He scrawled his signature on the license and handed it to his secretary to do the same as the witness.

"You so owe me for this," Stowe said to Wyatt.

Wyatt nodded and mumbled a thanks. "Make those calls I asked you to make."

Stowe returned the nod, and just like that, the couple exited the SUV, got back into their car and drove away.

The ceremony had lasted less than five minutes. Heaven knew how much time it would take her to get the annulment when this was over. And there would be an annulment. No way would she stay married to this stranger.

"What phone calls did you ask him to make?" Lyla wanted to know.

"He'll get the gossip mill going about our marriage. I want everyone to hear about it so the danger will end."

Maybe that wouldn't take long, and while she was hoping, Lyla hoped she could get close enough to that blood spatter to learn something. Because if Wyatt's plan failed, then her best shot was learning the identity of Webb's killer. And she was betting it was the same person who'd put her in harm's way.

Wyatt reached in his shirt pocket and extracted a simple gold wedding band.

Lyla was sure her mouth dropped open. "You took the time to buy me a ring?" But then she had a horrible thought. "It's not Ann's?"

"No. It belonged to Kirby's grandmother. I asked him if I could borrow it. Didn't say why, but I'll owe him and the others an explanation soon."

So, it was a family ring for something that usually meant the start of a new family. Too bad they'd made a mockery of the vows. But then she mentally shrugged. After two failed relationship, including one where she'd become a punching bag for her moronic ex, she'd given up altogether on the notion of marital bliss.

She was pretty sure there'd be no bliss in the sham one, either.

"Put on the ring," Wyatt instructed. "And make sure everyone sees it." Once the JP's car was out of the way, he started driving toward the facility. "We'll have to try to make people think we're newlyweds."

Lyla was almost afraid to ask what that might involve. And she was equally riled that her body seemed somewhat amused at the idea of playing a wife to Wyatt.

Get a grip.

Yes, he was attractive. Literally, he was the best-looking

man she'd ever laid eyes on, but she had to get her mind on ending the danger and not focus on the physical attributes of her fake husband.

Wyatt pulled to a stop in front of the building, where a group of vehicles were parked. One was the county CSI van. She knew the people who worked there, so she might see a friendly face. The sheriff's cruiser was there, too, along with a sleek silver car.

The moment they stepped from the SUV, a lanky dark-haired man came out of the building and started toward them.

"Billy," Wyatt greeted.

Billy Webb. The son of the man who'd been murdered. He no doubt knew he was a suspect, and that Wyatt might not trust him, because he lifted his hands to show them that he had no weapon.

Well, no visible one anyway.

His coat was plenty big enough to conceal a weapon or two.

"This is my wife, Lyla," Wyatt said, making introductions.

Billy tipped his head. "Mrs. McCabe."

She flinched before she could stop herself, but she didn't think Billy noticed, because he was already turning to go back inside. If he had any reaction whatsoever to the marriage, he didn't show it. Maybe that meant they could rule him out as a suspect in this manipulation-of-evidence plot.

Of course, maybe he was just a good actor.

"You remember the way to Stella's room?" Billy asked Wyatt.

Wyatt's gaze slid over the dingy walls and floor. "I remember everything about this godforsaken place."

Billy made a sound of agreement. They went through
the main area and up the stairs and into a wide side corridor. "And now I'm betting someone is trying to set Stella
up for Dad's murder," Billy added.

"You don't think she did it?" Lyla asked, earning herself a glare from Wyatt.

Probably because he didn't want her to say anything
that would connect her with the Webb investigation. Then
again, this was Wyatt, and even though she barely knew
him, he'd probably planned out every step of this visit.
And this conversation.

"No. I don't think Stella's guilty," Billy answered, and
he didn't hesitate, either. "I think it was someone associated with my dad's side businesses. In fact, I think that's
the person who talked my mother into putting the knife
in my dad's chest."

From what Lyla had read and what Wyatt had told
her, Sarah Webb did have an accomplice, but the woman
herself had instigated the killing. Of course, anything
was possible, especially since Sarah was emotionally
unstable. The product of years of physical abuse. Lyla
had gotten only a taste of it, and she knew how it could
batter a woman's soul and confidence.

"By side businesses, you mean the gunrunning your
father was doing with Travis Weston?" Wyatt asked.

"Yeah. But there doesn't seem to be any proof to link
Travis to the crime."

Wyatt didn't say anything about the gunman who was
connected to Travis, so Lyla didn't bring it up, either.

"What about the boys your father used?" Wyatt continued.

"The Rangers have checked. No records for that, of
course, and the only names I could remember were Da-

kota Cooke and Spenser Cash. Dakota died a few years ago in a car accident. Spenser has dropped off the radar."

That sounded some alarms in her head. Wyatt had called these events a pattern, and she was beginning to agree. It seemed awfully suspicious that one possible witness was dead and another missing.

They turned down another corridor, where there was a string of doors, all closed except for one, and a Texas Ranger was standing guard outside it.

Stella's room, no doubt.

"Who all lived here in this wing?" she asked.

"The help. Stella, the cooks and the housekeepers." Wyatt pointed to the doors at the end. "That was the Webbs' quarters at the time of the murder." He pointed to the door near it. "And that was his office."

Where it was believed the murder had taken place. Well, until now anyway. If Lyla remembered correctly, there'd been some spatter detected there, too, but it hadn't been enough to determine that Webb had actually died there.

"Stella has motive?" Lyla asked Wyatt.

"Yeah. I guess. Declan's her son, and Webb had beaten the hell out of him that day."

"He'd beaten a lot of people that day," Billy mumbled a split second before they stopped in front of the Ranger.

"Tucker McKinnon," the Ranger said. "You're Marshal McCabe, and I can't let you into this room."

Wyatt nodded. "This is my wife, the new director of the San Antonio Crime Lab."

"Your wife?" the Ranger questioned. His forehead bunched up. "Until I get word otherwise, I can't let her in, either."

But Lyla didn't need to get in. She just needed a look. And she got an eyeful. The UV light was still on the blood spatter that someone had tried to cover with paint, and the other tech was photographing it.

It certainly looked like a cast-off pattern to her, but there wasn't a lot of it. And the pattern would indicate only a single blow from the killer.

"Tell me about the spatter found in Webb's office months ago," Lyla said to no one in particular.

It was Billy who answered. "There was blood on the windowsill, the nearby wall and the floor. It appeared as if someone had tried to clean it up."

Interesting. Two areas of spatter and maybe someone had tried to conceal both. "Could the spatter have been caused by someone of your mother's height?"

Billy hesitated, then nodded. "She's about as tall as you are. Maybe a little shorter."

"Well, I don't think that's consistent with your mother's height." She tipped her head to the droplets on Stella's wall. "Or with Stella's. Of course, I can't be positive without actually examining it, but it looks as if this cast-off was created by someone taller. Someone at least six feet."

"Did you find any blood on the floor?" she asked the CSI who glanced in her direction.

He was young, and she didn't know him, but maybe because she was standing in between a marshal and a Texas Ranger, he answered anyway with a head shake. "In fact, this is the only blood we've found in the room," he added.

Since no one objected, Lyla tried a different question. "Can you determine how long ago the paint was put over the blood?"

"My guess is shortly afterward. It has the same amount of dust as the rest of the walls."

So, if the blood was from the time of the murder, then

someone had likely done a quick cover-up. Of course, that wouldn't have been hard to do. From what she'd read, no one had reported Webb missing for a full day. Plenty of time for a paint job.

She looked back at Wyatt. "How many of your suspects are over six feet tall and how many of them would have had access to this room?"

"Not Stella. But Kirby. With the exception of my youngest brother, Declan, the rest of us were already that tall."

"I was, too," Billy volunteered. "A lot of the boys were. But they wouldn't have come here often unless they were going to my dad's office. We weren't allowed in the staff's rooms."

That didn't mean it hadn't happened. A lot of rules had been broken here. "How about suspects who weren't residents? How many fit the height description?"

"Travis Weston," Billy and Wyatt said in unison.

Mercy, the circumstantial evidence just kept coming. But circumstantial wasn't going to hack it in this case, because they had volumes of it already. What they needed was to pinpoint a single, solid suspect so they could focus on stopping him.

She moved back from the Ranger, and both Billy and Wyatt followed her to the other side of the hall. "If that turns out to be Webb's blood," she whispered, "and none is found on the floor, then the investigator will likely conclude that the attack started in this room."

Wyatt glanced around, obviously considering that. "And then Webb went to his office, where Sarah finished the job?"

"Maybe." It was impossible to tell without testing both areas of spatter, something she was itching to do.

"There were traces of blood here on the floor." Billy

motioned from his dad's office to the stairs. "It appeared that he was dragged."

Not good. "The drag marks from his office could have obstructed or even destroyed the ones leading from Stella's room to his office." It was a wide hall, but two people dragging a body would have taken up most of the floor space.

Wyatt mumbled some profanity. "So, you're saying that maybe Sarah didn't have an accomplice for the actual murder, just someone after the fact to help her dispose of the body."

"That's exactly what I'm saying. And whatever investigator they name could likely say the same."

That, in turn, would implicate not only Travis but Kirby, too. Along with Wyatt and the majority of his brothers. Anyone could have helped Sarah drag her husband from the office and out of the building.

"There were no surveillance or security cameras, right?" she asked.

Wyatt shook his head. "And the visitors' log is missing. Which points to an outsider. Like Travis."

Kirby, too. But she kept that to herself. Wyatt already knew anyway.

However, Wyatt had a point about this maybe being an outsider. *If* the missing visitor's log was indeed connected to the murder. After all, the children who lived there wouldn't have signed in and out. But someone like Travis would have, and if he'd visited Rocky Creek at the time of the murder and if his name had been in the log, he would have made sure it disappeared. Which meant it wasn't just missing.

It'd likely been destroyed.

"What about this tape or recording your mother mentioned?" Wyatt asked Billy. Wyatt turned to her. "Sarah's been coming in and out of a coma, and she mumbled something about a tape."

"Still no sign of it," Billy insisted. "But she keeps talking about it. In fact, it's the only thing she has said so far. She opens her eyes, asks me about the tape, and then slips back into the coma."

That also got Lyla's attention. "What specifically does she say about the tape?"

Billy lifted his shoulder. "Only those two words— *the tape*."

So, not enough to tell them what the woman meant, but it had to be important for her to use what little conscious time she had to bring it up.

The Ranger's phone rang, the sound shooting through the hall. Seconds later, Wyatt's phone rang, too. And so did one of the CSIs'.

That put Lyla on instant alert, and she watched and waited as Wyatt looked at the screen. "Declan," he answered a moment later.

She couldn't hear what his brother said to him, but she had no problems hearing the Ranger. "Get out!" he shouted. "Someone just reported a bomb in the building."

"It's probably a hoax," Wyatt added. But he took her by the arm and got them running back toward the stairs. Billy and the others were right behind them.

"The evidence," Lyla reminded the Ranger. This could be an attempt to get them away from that blood spatter so that someone could tamper with it.

"I'll secure the building once everyone is out," Ranger McKinnon assured her.

They barreled down the stairs, with Wyatt still gripping on to her arm, but he stopped when he got to the front door, and he looked out. Only then did Lyla realize this could be a trap to lure them out into the open.

"Stay behind me," Wyatt insisted, and he drew his gun.

He maneuvered them to the porch and then made a beeline for his SUV. The others scattered toward their vehicles, as well. However, they'd barely made it inside the SUV when there was the horrible sound that shook not just the truck but the ground itself.

The sound of the blast.

"Get down!" Wyatt ordered, but he didn't wait for her to do that. He pushed her onto the seat and followed on top of her, shielding her with his body.

Lyla caught just a glimpse of the explosion as it ripped through the building and sent a spray of bricks and debris right at them. It pelted the SUV, but somehow the window held.

Cursing, Wyatt took out his phone while he kept his gun ready. "You need to get the fire department and bomb squad out here now," he said to whoever he'd called. No doubt one of his brothers. "Someone just blew up Rocky Creek."

Lyla lifted her head a little, praying that some part of the building was intact. And it was. But it wouldn't be for long.

The blast had made a gaping hole in the center of the bottom floor, but it'd also created a fire, and it was spreading fast. The fire department could likely save some of it if they got there in a hurry. But the smoke and the blast would almost certainly destroy or compromise any evidence inside.

"We're getting out of here." Wyatt moved back behind the steering wheel and started the engine.

He spun the SUV around and hit the accelerator. Lyla looked behind them at the wreckage, and her heart sank.

Not for the lost evidence, but for how close they'd come to dying. *Again.* They'd barely made it out of that building before the blast.

Wyatt hit Redial and then the speaker on his phone, and she heard Declan answer. "Who phoned in the bomb threat?" Wyatt asked.

"Anonymous call to the marshals' service from a disposable cell. Did everyone get out all right?"

"I think so. Who knew about the evidence that'd been discovered?"

"I'm checking on that now. You're thinking that was the motive?"

But Wyatt didn't answer. His attention was fixed on the road ahead, and when Lyla followed his gaze, she spotted the truck.

Not the justice of the peace.

But judging from Wyatt's profanity, it was someone he recognized. And didn't want to see. His grip tightened on his gun.

"I'll call you back," he said to Declan. "Travis Weston just showed up at Rocky Creek."

Oh, mercy. Travis was their prime suspect in this mess of an investigation.

Lyla studied the man, but she didn't think she'd ever met him. Tall, wide shoulders, and even though his hair was iron-gray, he didn't look old.

He looked formidable.

Wyatt brought the SUV to a stop because he had no choice. There were deep ditches on each side of the road, and Travis had parked his truck at an angle so they wouldn't be able to get by.

"Stay down," Wyatt warned her.

But he didn't take his own advice. With his gun ready,

he stepped from the SUV and took aim at Travis. "What do you want?"

Travis pulled back the side of his coat to reveal a gun in a shoulder holster. "Marshal McCabe, I understand we have a score to settle."

Chapter Seven

The last thing Wyatt wanted was this confrontation. Yeah, he would love to interrogate Travis and force him to talk, but he sure as heck didn't want to do that with a bomber in the area.

Especially since Travis or one of his cronies could be the one who'd set the explosive that'd been used to blow up Rocky Creek.

Wyatt kept cover behind the open door of the SUV, and he aimed his gun at Travis. "Why are you here?"

"A little bird told me this is where I'd find you. Since I didn't figure your ranch hands would let me near you, I decided to take a little drive so we could have a chat."

"Better make this conversation fast," Wyatt warned him. "Pretty soon this place will be crawling with cops and firemen. And Ranger McKinnon will want to *chat* with you, as well."

"The Ranger can wait. This is between you and me."

Wyatt first checked on Lyla to make sure she was staying down on the seat. She was, though she had that look of terror on her face again. He hated that there was nothing he could do about it. Two attacks in one day weren't going to give her any peaceful memories.

He tipped his head to what was left of the building behind them. "Your handiwork?" Wyatt asked Travis.

"Hardly." If he was insulted by that, Travis didn't show it. "I've got no reason to blow up things."

"Really?" And Wyatt didn't bother to take the sarcasm out of it. "Because I'd think finding new evidence would make you do something desperate. And you're here. Makes me wonder if you wanted to see your handiwork in action."

Travis shrugged as if he didn't have a care in the world. But obviously he did, otherwise he wouldn't be here. "If I was guilty of anything, I'd be desperate. But I'm not."

"You sure about that?" Wyatt pressed. "Because it seems pretty desperate to me that you'd drive all the way out here just to talk to me."

"I consider it a necessary chat. I'm here to tell you to call off your lawmen dogs. I got people digging through my bank records, looking for a connection to some idiot who apparently took shots at you."

"Nicky Garnett," Wyatt supplied. "But, of course, you know that because he's your hired gun."

"I haven't worked with Nicky in ages, and he was never my hired gun. I just used him as a bodyguard a time or two. Call off your dogs," Travis repeated.

"Not until they find whatever's needed to put you behind bars." In the distance, he heard the sirens. Soon, both Travis and he would have to get off the road so the fire department could get to the scene.

"Marshal, I figure it won't be long before you're a wanted man," Travis taunted. "If you're not already. And I'm not talking about your pretty face and how the women fawn over it, either."

"Is there a point to this?" Wyatt snapped.

"There is. You bent some rules, huh? And the truth is, that so-called new evidence inside Rocky Creek was just as likely to implicate Kirby, Stella, you or any of your brothers as it was me."

Wyatt hoped that wasn't the case, but it could be. Especially Stella, since the blood had been found in her former quarters.

"If you're not behind these threats, then who is?" Wyatt asked. "And don't name Kirby, Stella or anyone else related to me. I want the name of a real suspect."

"Hey, I can give you two. Sheriff Zeke Mercer and his business partner, Greg Hester."

They certainly weren't new names to Wyatt, and this wasn't the first time Wyatt had heard of them being associated with Webb's murder. They had already been questioned, of course, but there'd been no red flags.

"Why those two?" Wyatt pressed.

Travis made a sound to indicate the answer was obvious. "What better person to help cover up a crime than the sheriff, and Zeke was the first lawman on the scene after Sarah reported her husband missing."

"But Webb and Zeke were close friends," Wyatt pointed out.

"Friends don't always do friendly things," he mumbled. "The way I remember it, Zeke was mighty riled when he learned Webb was doing business with me."

"Riled because the business was illegal, like gunrunning?"

"Or maybe just 'cause it was cutting in on the illegal junk Zeke had Webb doing for him."

Wyatt tried not to look too surprised. "You're saying Zeke's dirty?"

"Hell yeah. I'm the one everybody suspected of doing something wrong at my own ranch, but doing something wrong is a heck of a lot easier if you're wearing a badge."

Wyatt huffed. "You want me to believe that Zeke set up the gunrunning at your ranch?"

He gave Wyatt a flat look. "Now, for me to admit to that, I'd have to admit I knew it was going on. And even if I learned it after the fact, I'd have to try to explain why I didn't report it. So, Marshal, I'm not admittin' anything."

"Then you're wasting my time." Wyatt started to turn and leave.

"No. Not if you hear what I'm saying, and I'm telling you to look at somebody other than me. Trying to pin Webb's murder on me is just plain dangerous. Not just for you but for your new bride, Lyla Pearson." Travis's eyes narrowed. "Yeah, I heard about your marriage already."

"That little bird you got is awfully chatty," Wyatt growled. And soon to be silenced, if Wyatt found out who it was. He didn't mind the marriage news being spread around—he wanted that—but Wyatt didn't want the same for Lyla's and his whereabouts.

"I figure you broke a few more laws to make those vows happen," Travis challenged. "Again, that's dangerous."

Now it was Wyatt who narrowed his eyes. "Is that a threat?"

"It's a warning for both of you." Travis turned to get back in his vehicle.

"The Ranger will want to talk to you," Wyatt reminded him.

"He knows where to find me. I'll be out at my ranch."

"Tell everyone that Lyla's out of this game," Wyatt called out to the man. "She has nothing to do with this investigation."

Travis stopped, spared him a glance. "Now, who would I tell that to? Just because you married her, it doesn't mean she's your wife. At least, not in the way that truly matters. And it doesn't mean she'll get a free pass on this."

The man smiled before he got into his truck.

Wyatt wanted to punch that smile right off his face. But he had enough to do without adding a fistfight. Too bad, since he knew he'd win. He never lost fistfights.

Travis drove out in reverse to get back onto the main road. Wyatt had to jump in his truck and do the same.

"You think he set that explosive?" Lyla asked the moment they drove away.

"Maybe. Or maybe he's just a jerk."

Unfortunately, Wyatt might not even get a chance to question him. But Ranger McKinnon would, and Wyatt hoped the lawman was good enough to spur some kind of confession.

But there was another possibility here.

Billy.

Wyatt didn't like the timing of the man's visit to Rocky Creek and the discovery of that blood evidence. Had Billy known all along it was there, because his mother had told him? If so, Billy could be using it to try to clear his mother's name and pin the murder on Stella. After all, Billy had said his mother might be coming out of the coma soon, and he wouldn't want her going to prison for the rest of her life.

"What about the other two Travis named, Sheriff Zeke Mercer and Greg Hester? Are they really suspects?" She shook her head. "I don't remember anything about them in the files I read."

"Because there wouldn't have been much to read. Webb and the sheriff were friends, and Greg Hester has been in business with Sheriff Mercer for the past decade or more. They're cattle brokers." And both very well-off. Brokering has made them rich men.

Unfortunately, rich men could buy hired guns like the ones who'd been out at Lyla's place. They could also hire someone in the medical field to steal an embryo and make sure it got in the person who could do them the most good.

Even though Wyatt needed to keep watch, he glanced at Lyla to make sure she was okay. She wasn't. There wasn't just the fear and the adrenaline on her face this time, but no doubt the realization that she'd made a huge mistake going through with this sham of a marriage.

She drew in a long breath, then another. "Travis made it sound as if our marriage wouldn't get me out of danger."

He had. And Wyatt wasn't sure what Travis had meant. But he'd find out.

"Keep watch around us," Wyatt told her, and while he did the same, he took out his phone to call Declan.

"What did Travis want?" Declan immediately asked. "Are you all right?"

"We're fine. He just told me to back off. No fists or bullets exchanged." Wyatt didn't spell out Travis's warning, but Declan no doubt picked up on it. "He said we should look at Sheriff Mercer and Greg Hester. Anything come up about them recently?"

"Not that I know of, but I'll check."

"Thanks. But maybe Travis is just blowing smoke." Or setting bombs.

"Is it true?" Declan said before Wyatt could continue. "Did you really get married to the new director of the San Antonio CSI?"

"I did. Her name is Lyla Pearson." And while Wyatt

needed to explain why he'd done what he had, he didn't want to do it over the phone. "We'll talk soon."

"Better be sooner than soon," Declan warned. "Stella and Kirby know. Saul, too. In fact, he was just talking to me about it when you called."

Well, good news did travel fast. That was good, *if* it stopped the danger. Saul was the head marshal, and Wyatt's boss, and he was also someone Wyatt would have liked to have told in person. Later, he was sure his boss would have a ton of questions, as would Wyatt's own family.

"What'd you need me to do?" Declan asked.

Wyatt mumbled a thanks to his brother for not pressing him on the marriage details. Because there were plenty of other things on their plate. "Ranger McKinnon needs to know about Travis's visit to Rocky Creek. He was there the same time as the explosion, which automatically makes him a suspect in the bombing. See if the Ranger will let Saul interview Travis."

Saul was maybe someone that the Rangers and governor would trust to do a simple interview. That way, Wyatt or one of his brothers could observe and even feed their boss some questions. That wouldn't necessarily happen if the Rangers ran the show.

"Billy needs to be questioned, too," Wyatt added. Even though Wyatt had no idea why Billy would destroy evidence that might help his mother's case. Unless… "Maybe you can find out if Billy had some kind of rift with his mother before she went into that coma."

"I'll try. Where you headed now?"

"The ranch." Wyatt paused. "Lyla's with me."

"Good." Declan paused, too. "Look, I don't know the reasons you married her, but there could be a problem.

Saul's already gotten a phone call from the governor about it."

Whoever was behind this had some serious contacts. Something that Wyatt needed to give some additional thought. "What'd the governor have to say?"

"Well, he wasn't pleased." Declan mumbled some profanity. "He wants Saul to find out if the marriage is real. And if it's not and if you did this to somehow manipulate whoever will be doing this investigation, then the governor wants you arrested for obstruction of justice. Not just you but Lyla, too."

Now it was Wyatt's turn to curse.

"So, my advice is this," Declan went on. "When you get to the ranch, you introduce everyone to your new bride. And make it convincing."

Oh, that should be fun. Lying to his family while pretending to be a happy couple.

"The best way for you two to stay out of jail is to convince everyone that you're real honest-to-goodness newlyweds," Declan added. "Put Lyla in your bed and keep her there."

Chapter Eight

Lyla was past having second thoughts about this so-called marriage, and those doubts got even worse when she stepped from the bathroom and spotted Wyatt. Before she'd left him to take a shower, he'd warned her that he wasn't going anywhere, that they'd be sharing his bedroom until the danger was over.

Well, he was true to his word.

He was on his bed, lying sideways. Still dressed.

For the most part anyway.

He'd taken off his holster and put it on the nightstand, but he'd unbuttoned his shirt while he talked on the phone. Something he'd been doing almost nonstop since they'd arrived at the ranch. He was obviously getting updates on the investigation, but those calls had done something else. They had prevented him from having more than a brief conversation with his family.

And with her.

However, he had taken the time to relay to her what Declan had said. That Wyatt should put her in his bed and keep her there.

Lyla hoped that wasn't a suggestion for them to have sex.

But then she rethought that.

Seeing Wyatt's bare chest and handsome face was

enough to spur her imagination in a really bad direction. He was certainly an eyeful. The stuff of fantasies and dreams, with that toned body. Not muscles from gym equipment, either. That was a cowboy's body.

If this marriage had been real, they'd be on a honeymoon, and she'd be on that bed with him. Her body went all soft and warm, clearly trying to push her to do just that.

She pushed back.

Consummating this marriage would be a disaster. Yes, it would no doubt be good.

No doubt.

But Wyatt and she had enough complications in their relationship without adding that. Besides, the attraction was probably one-sided on her part. Yes, she'd seen some heat in his eyes when he'd looked at her, but she figured a man like Wyatt looked at every woman that way.

He finished his call and sat up, his gaze zooming right in on her. First her face. Then, the bulky T-shirt she was using for a gown.

His T-shirt.

When she'd first put it on, she felt as if it swallowed her, but now she felt as if it skimmed way too much of her body.

Wyatt continued that sliding glance from the shirt to her bare feet and legs. "Tomorrow, I'll have someone pick up your things from your house."

She nodded and wished that she had a chastity belt for someone to retrieve. Or body armor. But even that might not be enough to stave off this heat.

Darn hormones.

He got up from the bed as if he didn't have a care in the world. Easy and slow. The movement caused his shirt to shift, and she got an even better look at his chest. Like his face, it was a winner. Toned and tanned and sprin-kled with dark coils of chest hair. Until that moment she hadn't realized just how attractive that sort of thing was.

Of course, maybe it wasn't, on any other man.

Her body seemed fixed on this one.

"Nerves?" he asked.

And it took her a moment to realize she was nibbling on her bottom lip along with staring at his chest.

She nodded. "Sharing a bed isn't a good idea."

He lifted his shoulder, shifting the shirt again. Mercy. He had a great stomach, too, but then what had she ex-pected? The man probably didn't have a flaw.

Well, not a physical one anyway.

But he had come up with a plan that basically sucked. Even he would probably agree with that right now. Be-cause despite that calm exterior, he had to be thinking of the logistics of close quarters with a woman who was clearly attracted to him but wanted no part of him.

Yes, this would be an interesting night.

"I agree," he said. "Sharing a bed probably isn't wise." His voice, like his motions, was slow and easy. But maybe that was her imagination. Everything about him suddenly seemed way too interesting.

Wyatt tipped his head to the floor on the other side of the bed. Lyla had to step around to see the pillow and covers he'd put there.

So, no bed sharing.

That was good, even though her own body seemed to have a different notion about that, too.

"Any updates on the bombing?" she asked. Best to get her mind on something other than Wyatt, and it wasn't as if they had nothing to discuss.

"All of this is just preliminary, but it appears the de-vice had been set outside the building on an exterior wall just below Stella's room. It was on a timer so it could have been put there hours earlier. Or days."

Lyla tried not to groan. "Are there security cameras?"

Wyatt shook his head. "No guard, either. The building was locked, though."

Of course, that hadn't stopped the bomber. "What about the evidence? Any idea yet how much was lost?"

His mouth tightened, and she knew the answer before he even said it. "The CSIs got out with the photos they'd taken, but pretty much everything else is gone. The building collapsed shortly after the fire department arrived."

Mercy. That meant the explosive device had been extremely powerful, and she shuddered to think how close they'd come to dying.

"Yeah," Wyatt said. He went closer, touched her arm with just his fingertips and rubbed gently. "But Declan thinks the bomber was the one who phoned in the threat."

So, he'd wanted them to get out. But why?

"More questions, few answers," he said when she made a sound of frustration. "I'm getting a little tired of that, too."

He drew back his hand from her arm, and Lyla hated that she was disappointed. Touching, even as a comforting gesture, was a big no-no with this sexual energy sizzling through the room.

"What about our situation?" Lyla asked. She saw the flicker of heat go through his eyes and realized she should clarify. "The possible charges for obstruction of justice?"

"Oh. That." Another shrug. "As long as we appear to have a marriage, there isn't much the governor can do. There's no physical evidence to link me to information

I found out about you. There are no records of the donor embryo or the theft at the fertility clinic storage."

"You destroyed it?" she asked.

"No. But someone else did."

Lyla pulled in a hard breath. What the heck was going on?

Wyatt made a sound, as if agreeing with her reaction, and he checked the time. "I need to grab a shower. The door's locked, and the security system's on." He pointed to the windows of the second-floor room. "Even the windows are wired for security, and if someone manages to get close enough to break the glass, the alarm will sound."

Good. Even though Lyla hated that these precautions had to be taken.

"When I'm in the shower, I want to leave the bathroom door open," Wyatt added. "Just in case."

Just in case there was an attack.

He didn't wait for her to agree, probably because he knew she had no choice, and he gave her arm another of those fingertip brushes before he headed into the bathroom.

And yes, the door stayed open.

Lyla made sure her attention was anywhere but on Wyatt undressing, but her imagination was too good tonight, and she saw him anyway. Not just the undressing. But as Wyatt stepped into the shower and let the steamy, hot water slide over his body.

Get a grip.

Her heart was racing. Her breath thin. All normal reactions if this were a real honeymoon night.

She snatched up her phone to get her mind on something else. No messages, but there were plenty of emails. Work was stacking up, but she'd already called the captain at San Antonio P.D. and explained why she couldn't come into the lab. Of course, he'd already heard about the attacks.

Had no doubt heard about the governor's concerns, too.

So, no one was pushing her to return to work, but soon a decision would have to be made. Either her cases would have to be reassigned or she would be replaced.

That felt like a fist around her heart.

She'd been a crime scene analyst since graduating from college seven years ago. She loved what she did, helping to solve cases that would clear the innocent and help convict the guilty.

But all of that could be taken from her.

She heard Wyatt turn off the shower and purposely kept her back turned, though she could hear him dressing. Except, he didn't really dress, Lyla soon learned when he stepped back into the room. No shirt, bare feet and he had on a pair of gray boxers that dipped precariously low on his waist.

Her mouth went dry.

Which was good, since she couldn't blurt out something stupid about his making a top-notch underwear model. Except somehow, wearing just the boxers, he still managed to look like a cowboy lawman.

Probably because of the scars.

She counted three. One on his upper right forearm. Another on the left side of his chest. And the other on his hip bone.

"Sorry, but I don't own pj's," Wyatt said.

Lyla tore her gaze from him and focused on her phone, which in no way needed her attention. There was nothing new left to see there, but it beat gawking at Wyatt.

"Are the scars from gunshots?" she asked.

"Yeah. There's another on the side of my head. Just a graze that my hair covers."

Four wounds. Good grief. Stella had been right about the bullet-magnet label. She wondered if that was because he was truly unlucky or if he'd just stepped up to take more dangerous assignments than most. Considering the way he was protecting her, she figured it was the latter.

Wyatt did a phone check, too, but he'd no sooner glanced at the screen when it rang.

"Hell," he grumbled. "Sheriff Zeke Mercer."

One of their suspects, and considering it was past eleven in the evening, his call probably wouldn't be good news.

"It's late," Wyatt snapped when he answered. Thankfully, he put it on speaker so she could hear what the man had to say.

"Yeah, but I figured you were up, being a newlywed and all." His voice was like gravel, and he sounded riled to the core.

So, Zeke knew about the marriage, too. Probably the baby, as well. Which was a reminder of something else hanging over their heads. The lab test that Wyatt had ordered on the amniotic fluid. The test that would determine if she was truly carrying his child.

"Travis told you I got married?" Wyatt asked.

"Who else? That man's got a ten-gallon mouth. Said he mentioned my name to you when you asked who'd blown Rocky Creek to smithereens."

"Your name came up. So did your business partner, Greg Hester."

Zeke stayed quiet a moment, as if surprised by that. "Because Travis is trying to cover his own hide, that's why. But you and I both know I had no reason to want Jonah Webb dead."

Lyla thought of the gunrunning deals that had gone on years ago. The ones Travis hinted that Zeke had orchestrated. But she doubted the retired sheriff would admit to a crime like that. Still, there might be some old records to link him, and she made a mental note to do some checking. Sometimes, evidence from gunrunning turned up in other cases, and maybe she could cross-reference that. Of course, that would first mean having access to the crime lab and files. Lyla wasn't sure how much longer she'd have that.

"What about Greg?" Wyatt pressed. "Did he have a reason to kill Webb?"

"You'd have to ask him, wouldn't you? But if I did the math right, Greg would have been just a teenager back then. Of course, that doesn't rule him out. You and your foster brothers were teenagers, and you're all suspects."

Wyatt huffed. "Is there a purpose to this call? Because as you pointed out, I'm a newlywed with better things to do." And he slid her a glance that caused her skin to flush.

"There's a purpose. Travis's hired gun, Nicky Garnett, was holed up in a dirtbag hotel over in San Antonio. I called the locals. Doing my civic duty. But they got there too late. Or else there's some kind of leak that alerted him."

Lyla knew of no such leak, but it was possible. Equally possible that Garnett had just gotten lucky and evaded the police.

"Next time I spot Nicky, I'll be calling you," Zeke said to Wyatt. "You got a hell of a big reason to bring him in, since he's the one who took shots at you."

"I'd appreciate any tip I can get." But Wyatt didn't

look or sound very appreciative. It was clear he didn't trust this retired lawman. And Lyla didn't trust him, either. Still, if he could deliver Garnett to them, then the gunman could tell them who'd hired him to come after Wyatt and her.

"Be talking to you then," Zeke added before he ended the call.

Wyatt stared at his phone for several seconds. "There's only one of our main suspects who hasn't contacted me personally," he mumbled. And he made another call. "Declan," he said a moment later. "I think it's time we talk to Greg Hester. Can you set up something for first thing in the morning?"

Unlike the other call, this one wasn't on speaker, but Wyatt rolled his eyes. "All right, but not too early, for appearance's sake."

Oh, because Wyatt and she were on their honeymoon and they needed to continue that facade until the culprit was caught.

Wyatt ended the call with his brother but kept hold of his phone and went across the room to the light switch. "Need anything before we pretend to get some sleep?"

Lyla couldn't help it—she smiled. It was the second time Wyatt had managed to do that, and she realized it'd been a while since a man had brought a smile to her face. Of course, Wyatt seemed to have her number.

"You can turn off the lights," she told him, and she climbed into the bed. Lyla pulled the covers up to her neck despite the fact the room wasn't chilly. She needed all the protection she could get between her and Wyatt's half-naked body.

He groaned when he got on the floor, and she nearly asked if it was hard. But best not to bring up that word, either. Still, it was difficult to avoid it when she heard him toss and turn, no doubt trying to get into a more comfortable position.

Lyla hoped she didn't regret what she was about to offer.

"It's a king-size bed," she pointed out. "One of us could sleep on top of the covers."

He didn't wait even a second to debate that. Wyatt grabbed his pillow, put his phone on the nightstand by his holster, and he dropped down onto the mattress. There was at least three feet of space between them, but Lyla figured that was still much too close.

"Now we can pretend to sleep and not notice each other," Wyatt mumbled.

Just like that, he eased the tension rising in her body. The heat was there, too, of course, but it actually helped to get everything out in the open. They were attracted to each other, and they shouldn't be.

Lyla closed her eyes, praying for sleep, since she was past the point of exhaustion, but barely a minute had gone by before the phone rang. Not Wyatt's.

Hers.

Wyatt scrambled across the bed, and they looked at the screen together. Unknown caller.

Not a good sign.

"Answer it on speaker," Wyatt instructed, and he turned on his own phone's recorder function.

Lyla waited until he had his phone right against hers before she hit the answer button.

"Lyla," the man said, his voice practically echoing through the room. "You've probably been waiting to hear from me."

Wyatt and she exchanged glances, and there was just enough light filtering from the windows that she could see the lift of his right eyebrow, no doubt asking her if she recognized the voice. But she had to shake her head.

This was a stranger.

Or perhaps one of the hired guns. She hadn't heard either of them speak, so she couldn't tell if this was one of them or not.

"Who are you?" Lyla asked.

"My name's not important. The only thing that's important is for you to listen. Did you really think marrying Wyatt McCabe would stop me?"

"I don't know what you mean," she answered.

"Sure you do. You married him to get yourself taken off the case."

"We got married because we're in love," Wyatt lied.

The caller made a *yeah right* sound. "Well, you and your new bride have a decision to make. Except, it's not really a decision. Lyla still has access to the crime lab and all the files on the Webb murder investigation."

It wasn't a question. "My marriage to Wyatt will disqualify me from working that case."

"I don't want you to work it. I want you to remove anything that implicates an accomplice. *Any accomplice,*" he emphasized.

"Why?" Lyla demanded. "From what I can tell, the evidence doesn't point to a clear-cut suspect, and who knows, there could be something in the case files to establish your innocence. If you're innocent, that is."

"Since you're likely recording this, I'll neither confirm nor deny that. But since you're recording this, it means there'll be no misunderstandings about what you're to do. Only keep evidence that proves Sarah Webb acted alone when she murdered her abusive husband. Destroy everything else."

Her heart rate doubled. Wyatt had been right about

someone wanting her to tamper with the evidence. But Wyatt had thought their marriage would prevent that from happening. Not according to the caller, though.

"And if we choose not to break the law?" Wyatt snarled.

"That's easy. You'll both die."

And with that, the man hung up.

WYATT COULD FEEL the throbbing in his head before he was even fully awake. He blamed that on the hour or two—at most—of sleep that he'd managed to get after Lyla's and his lives had been threatened.

These continued threats riled him to the core. But there'd been nothing he or his brothers could do to end this latest one, since there was no way to trace a call made from a disposable or burner phone.

Declan had the recording—Wyatt had given it to him the night before after the last call—and Declan would use it to try to get a voice match, but Wyatt figured that it hadn't been their would-be killer on the phone.

No way.

He would have used a peon for that call so that his voice wouldn't be recognized.

Wyatt forced his eyes open and came face-to-face with a sleeping Lyla. She was close to him. *Very* close. She was on her side, her left leg slung over his. Her leg was bare, and the new position hiked up her T-shirt so he could see her panties.

Pink.

He hadn't taken her for the girlie-underwear type, but it probably wouldn't have mattered what she was wearing. She could have had on granny panties, and his body would have still reacted. And he reacted, all right.

He went rock hard.

Great. Just what he didn't need this morning.

He glanced at the clock on the nightstand. It was barely six, but he needed to get up and check for updates on the case. Wyatt inched away from her. Or that was what he planned to do, but the slight movement must have startled her.

Her eyes flew open.

And suddenly he was looking right into all those shades of brown.

"Oh," she mumbled as if remembering where she was. But she didn't back away. Lyla just lay there with her leg still positioned over his.

As the seconds crawled by.

Wyatt couldn't be sure what she was thinking. However, it was pretty clear what was on his mind, and her gaze drifted in the direction of his erection, which was now pressed against her stomach.

She opened her mouth as if she might say something, but she clearly changed her mind. Wyatt changed his, too. A couple of times.

Should he kiss her? Should he do the smart thing? Smart would be, well, smart. But he decided to go the stupid route and kiss her anyway.

Wyatt slid his hand around the back of her neck, pulled her closer and put his mouth on hers. He didn't push things by deepening the kiss, figuring Lyla would stop this. And maybe slap him straight into the next county.

But she didn't.

No stopping.

Definitely no slap.

He remained firmly in the county, pressed against her and kissing her.

She made a sound of pure pleasure. A pink girlie

sound that went through him like a lightning bolt. And Wyatt put that fire and heat into the next kiss.

Oh, man. She tasted good. Not like morning, but like something forbidden and hot. Which she was. His mouth didn't let him forget that, and neither did the rest of his reckless body.

He pulled her closer, deepening the kiss even more. Deepening everything else, as well, since her leg had stayed on top of his, and the new position put his erection right against those pink panties.

Not good.

Because he already had some raunchy thoughts. Morning sex was usually the best. But sadly, he didn't think time of day had anything to do with it. He just needed Lyla badly, and he did some bad things because of that need.

He ran his hand between them and under her shirt. Touching her. On her stomach and then making his way up to her breasts. No bra. Just his bare hand on her bare skin, which was warm and well past inviting.

The kiss continued. So did the touching, but Wyatt wasn't the only one playing this game. Lyla touched, too. Her hand sliding over his chest. Her finger, easing through his chest hair. He'd never considered that a sensitive spot on his body, but he had to rethink it. Her touch was fanning the flames and making him crazy.

She made that sound again. A silky moan of pleasure mixed with some surprise.

Yeah, he was surprised, too.

Surprised this was turning into full-blown foreplay. Surprised that it felt far better than it should have.

And it was that last thought that kicked him in the head and caused him to back off and think. They couldn't keep this up. Not with so little clothing between them, a good bed and semisleepy brains. It was a perfect storm for what would be great sex.

That both of them would regret.

It wouldn't take long for that regret to set in, and Wyatt tried to focus just on that. And not on what would almost certainly be the pure pleasure leading up to the regret.

Her breath was gusting now, and she was staring at him as if trying to figure out what to say or do. She started to defuse things by slipping her leg away from his. That helped a little, but her scent was still on him, and he could still feel the sensation of his fingers touching her.

"Sorry." Lyla had to clear her throat and repeat it for the word to have sound. "It's the pregnancy. My hormones are all messed up."

Wyatt glanced at her tightened nipples, which were highly visible with the cotton shirt pressed against them. "Hormones caused that?"

"And you." She added some mumbled profanity. "That's not a compliment. I'm always attracted to the wrong man. Two failed engagements prove that."

It stung a little to hear himself called the wrong man. Even if it was the truth. But the rest of what she said wasn't true at all.

"I think the only thing your two failed engagements prove is that you were smart enough to end things before they went too far."

Of course, here she was married to him. Temporarily anyway. But in her mind, things had probably already gone too far in a really bad direction. That's why she'd lumped him in there with the two other wrong men.

Wyatt suddenly wanted to punch both of those men.

And he didn't know why.

There was just a lot of dangerous energy simmering

inside him, and he didn't know where to aim it. He definitely couldn't aim it at another make-out session with Lyla, because this time he might not have the willpower to pull away from her.

"What about you?" she asked. "Other than your late wife, have you had any serious relationships?" But she frowned, moved away and pulled the covers over her. "Don't answer that. A few kisses don't obligate you to tell me your life story."

No, but it felt as though they did. If not his life story, he wanted to share something with her. "I haven't been involved with anyone long-term since Ann."

Her chin came down a fraction. Her eyebrows came up. "If that's true, it's not for lack of opportunities."

He thought maybe that was a compliment to offset the wrong-man zinger. "There have been opportunities," Wyatt admitted. "But I gave up casual sex about the same time I grew chest hair."

She laughed. It was smoky and thick, and it slid through him just as fast as the fire from that kiss. Still smiling, she climbed off the bed and started for the bathroom, but she came to a quick stop.

And glanced at the front of his boxers.

"Need a cold shower, or can I go first in the bathroom?" she asked.

"Go ahead."

Once she was out of his sight, his other *problem* might take care of itself. And if that didn't work, his conversation with Declan was sure to do the trick. Because by now Declan had no doubt set up the interviews with their suspects. In a few hours, Wyatt would need to face down the person who wanted Lyla and him dead. That was a surefire way to kill some of these lustful urges.

He hoped.

So far, nothing else was working.

Wyatt got up, grabbed a pair of jeans from his closet and pulled them on. A shirt, too. Best not to be half-naked when Lyla returned. But before he could even zip up, his phone rang. Probably one of his brothers, but considering the hour—and the fact that all but Declan thought he was on his honeymoon—this was no doubt something important related to the investigation.

Maybe they'd gotten lucky and the bomber had been caught. While Wyatt was wishing and hoping, he added that maybe this idiot who'd set the bomb had made a full confession so that the danger would be over.

But it wasn't one of his brothers' names on the phone screen. It was his boss, Saul Warner. Hell. Was Saul calling to say he was on the way to arrest him?

"We got a big problem," Saul greeted before Wyatt could even say a word.

"What's wrong?" And Wyatt wasn't sure he wanted to hear the answer. He was sick and tired of bad news, and especially bad news that put Lyla in more danger.

"Wyatt, there's been another murder."

Chapter Nine

Lyla followed Wyatt down the stairs while he continued his latest call, this one to the medical examiner. There'd been a flurry of them since his boss had phoned to tell him the bad news.

That Sarah Webb had been murdered.

The news hadn't just shocked Lyla, it had terrified her. This wasn't some bomb set to destroy evidence in an abandoned building. Sarah had been murdered while in a coma in her hospital bed. A place most people considered safe, but obviously the killer had gotten to her.

And silenced her for good.

Since Sarah had confessed to murdering her husband—along with having an accomplice—that information was now dead along with her.

"We must be close to learning the truth," Wyatt said when he finished his call. He shoved his phone back into his pocket. "Or the killer wouldn't have murdered Sarah."

True. Plus, Billy had said that Sarah appeared to be coming out of the coma. Her accomplice wouldn't have wanted that if he or she thought that Sarah would implicate them in the murder. The penalty for assisting in a murder was the same as doing the act itself. So, the accomplice was looking at a life sentence, or maybe even the death penalty if premeditation could be proven.

"Does this rule out Billy?" Lyla asked. "Because I don't see him killing his own mother, and I don't see Sarah naming him as her accomplice."

Wyatt made a sound of agreement and continued toward the back of the house. "But that doesn't get the others off the hook."

No. In fact, it made their three suspects, Sheriff Zeke Mercer, Greg Hester and Travis Weston, look even guiltier.

Of course, the same could be said for Wyatt's family.

And speaking of family, Lyla hadn't expected to find them all there in the massive eat-in kitchen.

They were everywhere.

At the table. The stove. Leaning against the counters. Even though they all seemed to be doing something, they all stopped and turned to look at Wyatt and her. It didn't take long for a collective hush to settle over the room.

A long hush.

Since Declan was the only one who knew the marriage was a sham, they were probably all thinking that either Wyatt had lost his mind or she'd somehow trapped him. After all, she couldn't be his usual type. They were probably used to him bringing home beauty queens and model types.

Lyla resisted the urge to make sure her ponytail and clothes were straight, but she wished she'd at least put on some makeup.

"Anything on the caller who threatened Lyla?" Wyatt asked Declan.

"Nothing." Declan made an uneasy glance around the room, as if bracing himself for someone to demand to know more about the marriage. When no one did, Declan cleared his throat and continued. "There's nothing in his voice or the background noise to indicate who he is or where he was when he made the call."

"You'll have to excuse our manners, but this is how crazy things get in the middle of an investigation," a very pregnant blonde said, walking toward Lyla. The woman hugged her. "Welcome to the family. I'm Joelle." She tipped her head to the lanky dark-haired man on one of the bar stools, who was talking on his phone. "Married to Dallas."

Wyatt continued the introductions from there. "Everyone, in case you haven't heard, this is Lyla, my wife." He hooked his arm around her as if remembering at the last minute they were playing the part of honeymooners.

There were several more moments of pin-dropping silence. A few odd looks, too. Even a whisper between one of the couples. Then, the chatter and activity continued as if a marriage announcement wasn't that unusual.

And maybe it wasn't.

Because Stella was the only one in the room who wasn't wearing a wedding ring.

Stella took a skillet of sizzling bacon off the stove and came over to give her a hug, too. "That's Harlan and Caitlyn," she said, pointing to the couple at the table. The woman was also pregnant and sitting so close to her husband that she was practically in his lap. They both added a welcome after looking up from papers they were studying.

"That's Lenora and Clayton," Stella continued. "And their precious little boy, Clay, Jr." She motioned toward the woman helping her in the kitchen and then to the man seated at the table next to Declan. Clayton was holding a sleeping baby only a few months old on his lap, and he glanced up from his computer, mumbled a welcome.

Declan managed a smile when he looked at Lyla. Forced, no doubt. And brief. He put his attention back on the laptop screen positioned in front of him.

"That's Kirby." And Stella's smile was genuine when her attention landed on the man in the wheelchair at the head of the table. Even though it was obvious that the man was recovering from a serious illness, he didn't look nearly as weak as Lyla had imagined he'd be.

"Welcome," Kirby greeted. He, too, had some papers on the table. "Wish it were under better circumstances. Still, we'll have time to celebrate soon."

Yes, soon, if they managed to identify and catch this killer. And after that, there'd be no need to celebrate the marriage, because Wyatt and she would be able to either tell them the truth or get an annulment. First, though, they had to stop kissing and doing other things that would lead to sex. Because even though she had no legal training, Lyla was pretty sure that sex would nix an annulment.

It would certainly make it harder for her to walk away from Wyatt, too.

"Slade, his wife, Maya, and their two boys will be here soon," Joelle finished. "And Declan's fiancée, Eden, is in her office, working. She's a P.I. and is trying to use her contacts to get a lead on the gunman Nicky Garnett."

Joelle leaned in closer to Lyla. "Bet you're wondering how we all fit in this room, huh? Especially with all the babies and pregnant bellies?"

Even though Joelle probably meant it as a joke, it had crossed Lyla's mind. This massive dose of *family* was past being overwhelming, especially since she'd been an only child, and her parents had passed away a few years earlier.

"You okay?" Wyatt whispered to Lyla the moment Joelle stepped away to join her husband at the breakfast bar. "You're looking a little pale."

"I'm okay," she lied. And she prayed the smell of that

bacon didn't trigger a bout of morning sickness. That would add another level of discomfort to this family gathering, and it would be darn hard to explain, since they didn't know about the pregnancy.

"What about Sarah's death?" Wyatt asked. "I was trying to talk to the medical examiner earlier, but he was tied up. Do we know yet how she was killed?"

Declan scrubbed his hand over his face. "No marks on her body, but something was injected into her IV. They're examining it now."

"Looks like it could be snake venom," Clayton said, reading from his computer screen.

"Sweet heaven," Lyla said under her breath. Some of the others responded with profanity, including Wyatt.

It was a first for Lyla. In all years of crime scene investigation, she'd never seen a case where snake venom had been used as a murder weapon.

"Once they know specifically what kind of venom was used," Clayton continued, "then we might be able to find the source."

True. There weren't many places in the state where someone could buy it. Of course, the killer could have hired someone else to do the job. If so, there wouldn't be a record, and judging from the dire expressions on Wyatt's brothers' faces, they had already come to that conclusion.

"What'll you have to start you off? Coffee or tea?" Stella asked in an attempt to change the gruesome conversation.

It might seem too obvious if she asked for milk, something she'd been drinking a lot of lately. "Tea, thanks. Black." Maybe she could hold that down.

"I'll get that for you. And if you're hungry, just help yourself to the bacon and eggs on the stove."

Lyla smiled. Thanked her. But Lyla knew she wouldn't be touching anything on the stove.

"Saul just got us the surveillance feed from the hospital," Declan said, drawing Lyla's attention back to him. "I'm looking at the hour and a half before Sarah's murder. Clayton's looking at the hour and a half after. If we don't find anything, we'll widen the time frame. It's possible her killer sneaked in earlier in the day."

And it was just as possible that it was a killer they wouldn't know, since he could be just another hired gun. For that matter, the person could have even used a disguise. She doubted anyone was bold enough to walk into a room and murder a woman when there was a good chance that someone would recognize him.

"Was there a camera outside her room?" Wyatt went for the coffeepot and poured himself a huge cup. He gulped down some, as if it were the cure to the headache he no doubt had. He also snatched a piece of bacon piled high on a platter.

"No camera there," Clayton answered. "The only ones inside the hospital are in the pharmacy and the emergency room."

Both places where crimes were the most likely to occur. "What about the exterior?" Lyla asked.

Declan nodded. "And that's what we're focusing on now. There are two cameras that cover both the back and front parking lots and all the entrances except for several of the clinic doors on the west side of the building."

"Anyone can go through those doors?" she pressed.

"No," Wyatt answered. "But anyone could break into them, especially since Sarah was killed after regular clinic hours."

Lyla groaned. It wasn't much of a stretch to believe a killer would also resort to breaking and entering to get to his soon-to-be victim. Added to that, it wouldn't have been especially hard to conceal a syringe filled with venom. It could easily fit into a pocket, unlike a gun that might be noticed.

Stella brought Lyla a steaming cup of tea, and even though there were empty seats at the table, she stood. Wyatt stayed next to her, though he continued to check his phone for updates while he wolfed down more bacon, which he sandwiched with some toast.

"I'm going over the report from the bombing," Harlan volunteered. "The bomb squad says it was almost certainly a professional job. They're hoping once they reconstruct the device, they'll be able to tell us who made it."

The bomb's signature. Lyla wasn't an expert in the area, but she knew someone who was. She nearly reached for her phone to call him but then remembered she wasn't in a position to be asking favors from former coworkers. In fact, she wasn't sure exactly what position she was in when it came to work, but she doubted it was a good one.

"So, what are we gonna do about this caller who threatened Lyla and Wyatt?" Kirby asked.

She looked at Wyatt, even though Lyla already knew the answer. "I won't tamper with evidence," she insisted.

"Wouldn't do any good anyway," Kirby concluded. "There's little chance this guy would just let you live afterward. You'd be a deadly loose end for him."

Mercy. She'd known that, of course, but it was hard to hear it said aloud. It didn't matter which way she went, she was in danger. And that included this marriage arrangement with Wyatt.

"I figure we'll just need to keep Lyla safe here at the ranch," Wyatt explained. "Of course, that means everyone else should stay away just in case."

Just in case bullets start flying.

Clearly that bothered Joelle, because she snuggled closer to her husband. Even though Dallas was reading something, he idly looped his arm around her and kissed her. The idleness vanished when he looked at her, and he kissed her again.

Lyla quickly glanced away. It was too private a moment. Except, her attention landed on Caitlyn and Harlan, and they were kissing, too.

"Ignore them," Wyatt whispered, following her gaze. "They've had the hots for each other since they were teenagers. Dallas and Joelle, too."

"What about them?" She tipped her head to Stella and Kirby, and even though they weren't kissing, Stella had leaned in, her mouth close to Kirby's ear as she whispered something.

"Them, too." Wyatt cursed under his breath. "It's possible we're the only ones on the ranch not having sex."

Lyla didn't dare laugh, because in this case, the truth hurt. Despite all the danger and the trouble that sleeping with him would cause her, her body was still aching from the memory of Wyatt's kisses.

"You should try to eat," Wyatt suggested, and he led her into the kitchen. Nothing looked good, and her stomach felt ready to clench at any moment, so she settled for a piece of dry toast that was sitting in the toaster.

"Bingo!" Declan said, getting up from his seat and turning the laptop to face their direction. The others quickly gathered around.

Lyla saw the image that was frozen on the screen, and it appeared to be the back parking lot of the hospital. It was littered with cars, but there was only one person visible in the shot.

A man wearing jeans and a white cowboy hat.

"Sheriff Zeke Mercer," Wyatt provided. "He was at the hospital."

Declan nodded. "And from the time stamp on the surveillance, he was there about one hour before Sarah was found dead."

That meant the former lawman had motive and opportunity. All that was left was the means, and to do that, they'd need to connect him to the snake venom.

"You got Sheriff Mercer," Harlan said. "Well, I got his business partner, Greg Hester." He turned the screen toward them, and Lyla saw the short blond-haired man getting into a black car.

"Greg didn't come with Zeke," Harlan added. "Because this footage was shot after Sarah had already been found dead."

"Run the footage," Wyatt insisted.

Harlan rewound and then hit Play, and it didn't take her long to see Greg coming out, not through a side entrance but the front. And he wasn't just walking. He was hurrying. Like a man on the run.

"Hell, what were they both doing there?" Wyatt asked, but he didn't wait for an answer. "Maybe they were in on it together."

"Maybe," Lyla agreed. "But wouldn't they have known about the security cameras?"

"They haven't been up in the parking lot that long," Declan explained. "Just a few months. Before that, there were only cameras in E.R. and the pharmacy."

She thought about that a moment. "What about Billy? Any sign of him?"

"Not so far," Declan said, and Harlan mumbled something similar.

"If Travis Weston shows up on that footage," Dallas said, "then they'll all claim they were set up."

They'd probably claim it anyway. And at least one of them would be lying. Well, unless Billy had somehow managed to do the unthinkable and kill his own mother.

"It's time one of you talked to all the suspects," Kirby advised. "You, too." His weathered eyes landed on Lyla. "If one of them is behind the threats, then it might do them some good to see you and Wyatt together. That way, they'll know he and all his brothers will be protecting you."

Lyla hadn't thought of things from that angle, that it might get the killer to back off if he thought she was well protected by a family of federal marshals.

Was that why he'd gone after Sarah instead?

Because she'd been vulnerable?

Or maybe he'd even wanted to send Lyla a message—that she could be next. Whatever his motive, she didn't want to be away from Wyatt anyway since he seemed bound and determined to protect her and the baby.

Lyla was counting heavily on that.

She wasn't a coward, had always fought her own battles, but fighting this one alone could cost her the baby. She'd rather rely on Wyatt than risk that.

"I'll make the calls," Dallas volunteered, "and have the suspects come to the marshals' office. Declan's arranged for Greg to be there, so we might as well get three birds with one stone." He checked the time. "Does an hour or two from now sound okay?"

Wyatt didn't agree right off. He looked at her, as if debating what Kirby had suggested.

"You want me to stay here while you talk to them?" she asked, knowing that wasn't going to happen.

"I'm not letting you out of my sight," Wyatt verified. "We'll just have to be smart about this. I don't want to take you into town unless I'm sure I can keep you safe."

And he moved away from her to start coordinating things with Dallas.

Lyla intended to stay out of the action, but both Caitlyn and Joelle came toward her. "They'll be a while," Joelle said, taking Lyla by the arm. "It'll give us a chance to talk."

That put a knot in Lyla's stomach, and she looked back at Wyatt to see if he could stop this, but his attention was on whatever Clayton was showing him on the computer screen.

Joelle and Caitlyn led her through the kitchen, snagging some food along the way, and they sat at a small breakfast table that faced the massive manicured backyard.

"All right." Caitlyn dished up some of the bacon and eggs for the three of them. "Spill everything. How'd you manage to snag Wyatt?"

Lyla realized she should have expected the question, but she didn't know how to answer it. Anything she could say would be a lie.

"Wait." Caitlyn shook her head. "I didn't mean it like that. *Snag* makes it sound like you tried to deceive him in some way. It's just that Wyatt never said anything about being involved with anyone, much less being in love."

"He's not exactly the baring-his-soul type," Joelle continued, "but we're surprised we didn't get a hint about the marriage before he just sprang it on us."

"It happened very fast," Lyla settled for saying.

Caitlyn smiled. "Love at first sight. The best kind. It's what happened with me when I first saw Harlan."

"Same here with Dallas." Joelle leaned in, lowered her voice. "But with the exception of Ann, Wyatt just hasn't jumped into any relationships. Before Ann, he was definitely the *love 'em and not hang around for long* type."

Lyla didn't doubt that. "How long have you known him?"

"About eighteen years," Caitlyn answered, and Joelle bobbed her head in agreement. "We all grew up together at Rocky Creek."

"I'm pretty sure you're the first woman he's brought home since his late wife," Joelle continued. "Of course, that's what happens when you're in love." She glanced over at him. "And it's pretty clear that he's crazy about you."

Lyla frowned and looked at Wyatt to see if Joelle and she were seeing the same thing. Obviously not. The only thing she saw on Wyatt's face was worry and concern while he was talking on his phone. If there was any craziness involved, it was only his obsession to keep her safe.

An obsession she was thankful for.

"So, when will you tell everyone you're pregnant?" Caitlyn asked.

Lyla's mouth dropped open. Either Wyatt and she were giving off some kind of weird vibes or else these two were mind readers.

"Uh, excuse me a second," Lyla said, hoping to get her out of answering that question. But she also wanted to see what had put that look on Wyatt's face.

He ended his call, but he stared at the phone for several seconds before his gaze met hers. There was something in his eyes that she couldn't interpret.

Wyatt didn't hurry when he came toward her, but as Joelle had done earlier, he gripped on to her arm and took her not just out of the breakfast area but through a formal dining room and to the other side of the house. He finally stopped when they reached the foyer, and he looked around to make sure they were alone.

They were.

"What happened?" she asked, and Lyla tried to brace herself for another death threat. Or worse, another murder.

Wyatt dragged in a long breath. "The test results are back."

With all the talk of the crime scene and bomb, it took her a moment to realize which test results he meant.

The one from her amniocentesis.

A test that would tell them whose baby she was carrying.

Chapter Ten

Wyatt hadn't thought beyond the test results. Hadn't even considered how to tell Lyla. But judging from the way she staggered back and caught onto the wall, she already knew what he was about to say.

"The baby's mine."

The jolt went through him. So did the memories of how Ann and he had planned and hoped for this baby. Of course, they hadn't planned on *this*.

But then neither had Lyla.

She'd planned to have her own baby. One that she wouldn't have to share with a birth father.

"You're sure?" she asked, but then she waved him off, and she moved away from him when Wyatt tried to take hold of her. She didn't look too steady on her feet.

And wasn't.

Groaning and with her back still pressed against the wall, she sank down to the floor and put her hands over her face.

Wyatt had no idea what to say to her. Not *I'm sorry,* because that would be lie. He'd desperately wanted this child to be his, and it was. But there was no joy in seeing Lyla fall apart like this.

"Everything you told me has come true." Her words didn't have much sound, and she was on the verge of crying. "The threats, the attempted blackmail." She paused, her mouth trembling. "Now the baby."

Wyatt stooped down and tugged her hands from her face so he could make eye contact. Why, he didn't know. He was probably the last person on earth she wanted to see right now, but he had to try to make this better.

Even if that was impossible.

Yeah, there were tears, all right, and even though Lyla was blinking them back, one still spilled down her cheek. Wyatt brushed it away with his thumb, but another quickly followed.

"I love this baby," she whispered on a hoarse sob.

"So do I." And that was a massive understatement. For both of them.

Lyla wanted this child enough to carry it and become a single parent. Definitely not an easy lifestyle choice. It'd be easier for him because he had a huge family ready and willing to help, but Wyatt didn't think Lyla would appreciate his bringing that up now.

She finally met his gaze. "You'll challenge me for custody." And it wasn't a question.

He would.

Except that didn't feel right, either.

After all, Lyla still had over six months to go to carry this child. He seriously doubted her love for the baby would lessen during that time. Just the opposite. And she'd be the one taking all the risks that came with the pregnancy.

"Maybe we can work something out," he offered.

"Shared custody." She shook her head. "You really want this baby starting out his or her—" Lyla stopped, froze, probably because she saw the look on his face. "The test would have given you the sex of the baby."

He nodded.

Wyatt didn't get to do or say more than that, because he glanced over his shoulder at the sound of footsteps behind him and he spotted Declan making his way toward them.

"Everything okay?" Declan asked.

Neither Lyla nor he answered, but Wyatt did help her to her feet.

"Two of our suspects are on their way to the marshals' office," Declan continued, studying Lyla. He'd no doubt noticed the tears she was still trying to wipe away. "Zeke and Travis."

Even though it was hard, Wyatt forced himself to think of the investigation and not the life-changing news he'd just delivered to Lyla.

"Did Zeke happen to say why he was at the hospital right before Sarah was murdered?" Wyatt asked.

"Not yet, but no one's there to question him yet, since Saul's had to leave town to testify at a trial over in Eagle Pass. It's just Zeke, Travis and the dispatcher until Harlan gets there. He just left. Ranger McKinnon's on the way, too, but he's still a half hour out."

Great. It wasn't a good idea for Zeke and Travis to be alone together, since they were both accusing the other of being involved with not just Webb's murder but the recent attacks. They might try to kill each other, and while Wyatt didn't care if they inflicted some bodily harm, he wanted them both alive so they could answer questions.

"Dallas and Clayton are staying here with the family," Declan continued. "Just in case." He didn't spell out there could be an attack, but all of them knew it. "Slade's out of pocket because he just got called out to pick up a fugitive. I'd like to head over to the crime lab so I can push for some headway on this bomb and study the other reports coming in."

All of that was necessary, but it left Wyatt to assist with the interrogations. Well, unless Saul pulled the plug on them before Wyatt could try to get whatever information he could out of Zeke and Travis.

"We should go," Wyatt told Lyla. "I don't want Harlan to have to tackle this by himself."

She nodded. Her crying had finally stopped but that was probably because Declan was there. Later, the tears would come and so would the inevitable discussion they'd need to have. He was betting that wouldn't lead to another round of kissing.

But Wyatt did brush a kiss on her forehead.

He wasn't sure it gave her much comfort, but it certainly helped him.

"Let me get my purse," she mumbled, and headed toward the stairs, leaving Declan there to stare at him.

Make that a glare.

"Are you trying to make this harder than it already is?" Declan asked. "Because there's no reason to do a loving-couple act around me."

"It's not an act." Wyatt winced at that. Then, cursed. "I mean, I'm attracted to her."

Declan's hands went on his hips. "Not exactly a news flash, brother. But what do you think this is doing to her, huh? She's already having to play the part of your wife, and if you find out the baby is yours—"

"It is."

Declan's glare melted away, and he squeezed his eyes shut a moment. "Like I said, don't make this harder on her than it already is."

Darn good advice. Wyatt hoped his body would listen. And his heart. Because with Lyla carrying his baby, it tore down even more walls between them. He wasn't ready for that to happen yet. Maybe never would be.

"Did something happen?" Lyla asked from the top of the stairs. She volleyed glances at both of them.

Wyatt shook his head and got them moving out the front door and into his SUV. He wanted to hurry so he didn't have to keep thinking about paternity tests and feelings. Better for him to concentrate on learning about what was going on. But he also had to be careful about another attack, so he watched their surroundings when he drove away from the ranch.

"What did Caitlyn and Joelle have to say to you?" he asked.

Lyla didn't jump to answer, and she gave him the same kind of look she'd given him when she'd seen him talking with Declan. She no doubt figured he was hiding something. And he was. He was hiding the fact that the baby news had clouded everything in his head, and the warning from Declan had just added to his confusion.

"Caitlyn guessed I was pregnant," she finally said.

That was not something he'd expected to hear. "How?"

Lyla shook her head. "I didn't say a thing, but maybe it takes one to know one. Or something like that." She groaned softly. "All of this pretense is a lot harder than I thought it would be. And pretty soon you'll have to tell them the truth about the marriage. About the baby."

Yeah, he would. Especially if his brother's wife had already figured out part of it. Still, it wasn't something he just wanted to blurt out, and he didn't want it to come in the middle of this dangerous mess. Of course, one way to end the mess was to get a confession from the person who'd orchestrated it.

Maybe Zeke or Travis.

But he didn't want those answers at Lyla's expense.

"You've already taken on enough stress," he told her

as he pulled into the parking lot of the marshals' building. "It's not good for you or the baby to add more, so you can wait in Saul's office while Harlan and I talk to these guys."

She didn't argue, didn't even make a sound, but then the same thoughts whirling through his mind were no doubt whirling through hers.

They went inside and through the security check, but before they even got up the stairs to the offices, Wyatt heard the yelling. When Wyatt stepped into the squad room, he saw Travis and Zeke with Harlan between them. His brother was definitely having to stave off a fistfight.

Wyatt grabbed Zeke by the collar just as Zeke brought up his fist, and Wyatt slung the man out of the fray. He didn't get any thanks from Zeke though for stopping him from trying to land a punch.

"He set this up!" Zeke threw off Wyatt's grip and jabbed his index finger in Travis's direction. Zeke's face was bright red, veins bulging on his neck, and his breath was coming out in ragged spurts.

Unlike Travis.

He didn't appear to be ruffled at all, but Wyatt figured that was just to rile Zeke even more.

"What'd he set up?" Wyatt demanded.

"Nothing," Travis answered, but Zeke had a different notion.

"He had some woman leave a message on my phone," Zeke fired back. "A woman pretending to be Sarah Webb. I kept the message, so you can listen for yourself."

"I already did," Harlan explained. "It's a woman, all right, and she called about an hour and a half before Sarah was murdered. But it could have been anyone. Her voice isn't louder than a whisper."

"Exactly the way a woman would sound if she'd just

come out of a coma." Zeke gave Travis another finger jab. "And he's the one who had her call me and ask me to come to the hospital, saying she had to talk to me right away. He knew I'd go running to the hospital and that it'd set me up for her murder."

Interesting. Wyatt wondered if Greg had gotten the same message. Of course, even if he had, it didn't mean Zeke and he were innocent. Because they could have had someone call them and leave the message so they'd *look* innocent.

Or maybe Sarah really had come out of the coma.

If she had, then the woman could have used the phone in her hospital room. It was a long shot, but Wyatt needed to see if there was a way to trace a call from there.

"The same woman called me," Travis volunteered. "I didn't save it, and I damn sure didn't go to the hospital. I figured it was some kind of setup."

"Yeah, because you're the one who set it up," Zeke snarled.

Since this argument could go on for a while, Wyatt looked back at Lyla. "Why don't you go ahead into Saul's office?"

"Your bride should stay," Travis insisted. "She might learn something to make you back off from trying to pin this on me."

"I'm not trying to pin anything on you," Wyatt insisted. "I'm trying to learn the truth."

Lyla did go to Saul's office, but she didn't close the door.

"If you want the truth," Travis went on, "then try this theory on for size. Years ago, Webb asked me to let some of the boys from Rocky Creek work on my ranch. But what he had in mind was gunrunning with his old friend, the sheriff here."

"You're admitting to this?" Harlan asked Travis.

"Just a theory." Travis's tone became even more smug. "And continuing that theory, something went wrong with the arrangement, and Webb and Zeke had a fallin'-out."

"You're a lying, worthless snake," Zeke argued. "And you're the one who had the fallin'-out with Webb, because he didn't know about the gunrunning. You set it all up, and when Webb confronted you about it, you helped Sarah kill him."

Travis just smiled. "Prove it. Oh, you can't, can you? Because you got no evidence."

"Other than your connection to the gunman who took shots at Lyla and me," Wyatt reminded him.

Oh, that narrowed Travis's eyes, and it got worse when Zeke chuckled.

Travis turned those narrowed eyes on Zeke. "It's not me on that surveillance footage. It's you." And Travis's smug look returned. "And I'm thinking you murdered Sarah because she might spill her guts and tell everyone you helped her kill her husband."

No angry outburst this time. Zeke just shook his head. "Sarah was my best friend's wife. I wouldn't have hurt her."

"But you think I did," someone said.

Wyatt cursed because he hadn't heard the footsteps behind him. Cursed even more that Greg, a suspect, had managed to waltz right in with Lyla so close.

"I don't think that," Zeke told Greg. He tipped his head to Travis. "I believe he set us up."

"Well, someone did." Unlike the other men, Greg was wearing a dark blue business suit. He definitely didn't look like a cattle broker. "I got a call asking me to come to the hospital." He pressed the speaker function on his phone. "Listen for yourself."

It only took a few seconds for the voice to pour through the room. "It's me, Sarah Webb," the woman said in a hoarse whisper. "I need to see you. I'm scared. Please don't tell anyone I'm out of my coma, because someone wants to keep me silent. Come to the hospital now but don't let anyone see you going into my room."

Wyatt checked the time of the call. A good half hour before Sarah had been found dead. "How'd you get into the hospital without being seen?"

"Clinic entrance," Greg said without hesitation. "One of the doctors was working late, I guess, because I saw a patient leave through that door, and I went in." He paused. "By the time I got to Sarah's room, she was already dead."

Wyatt studied Greg's body language but couldn't tell if he was lying. In fact, he couldn't tell much of anything, because Greg seemed completely unruffled by any of this.

"Did you see anyone?" Zeke asked him. "Like Travis, maybe?" He didn't wait for Greg to answer. "Because he could have gotten in the same way you did."

"I wasn't there," Travis insisted.

"I didn't see him," Greg said at the same time. "But that doesn't mean he wasn't there."

Lyla came out of the room, and even though Wyatt gave her a warning glance to go back, she stayed put.

"Why would Sarah have called you?" she asked Greg, taking the question right out of Wyatt's mouth.

"Greg's known Sarah for over a decade," Zeke answered. "Ever since we've been in business together. I took him with me more than once whenever I drove out to Rocky Creek to check on her."

Wyatt kept his attention planted on Greg, who suddenly looked uncomfortable. Or something. "That's true?" Wyatt motioned for Zeke to keep quiet.

"I knew Sarah," Greg finally said. At first, he dodged Wyatt's gaze, but then met him eye to eye. "Remember the two boys who Webb sent out to work on Travis's ranch?"

"Don't do this." Zeke tried to take hold of Greg's arm, but Harlan blocked him. Zeke continued to warn Greg, but he obviously ignored him.

"The ones he had gunrunning," Greg continued.

Wyatt nodded. "Dakota Cooke and Spenser Cash. Cooke's dead and Cash is missing."

"He's not missing," Greg said, and then he hesitated. "He's standing right in front of you."

Travis went closer, his attention pinned to Greg's face. "Well, I'll be damned. It's you, ain't it, boy? You're Spenser Cash."

Judging from Zeke's profanity, not only did he know it, but it was something he'd wanted to stay hidden.

Wyatt stared at Greg, trying to pick through the features to see if it was a face he remembered. He could see it now but only after the fact. Of course, he hadn't expected Spenser to change his appearance and identity, and Wyatt had even considered the guy might be dead.

"I've had a few surgeries. Changed my hair," Greg explained. "After Webb disappeared, someone tried to kill me. At first, I figured it was his gunrunning friends trying to tie up loose ends, so Zeke helped me change my identity."

"You knew all this time?" Harlan demanded, looking at Zeke.

The man nodded. "Greg was a good kid. And Kirby's not the only one who wanted to protect some of the boys there. I got Greg out of harm's way, and the person causing that harm is standing right there." He pointed at Travis again.

"I didn't try to kill him," Travis grumbled. "I didn't even know he was still alive until just this minute. And besides, I got no reason to want him dead."

"No reason other than trying to cover up the gun-running," Zeke argued. "Or covering up your part in Webb's murder."

"It might not have been Travis," Greg said, drawing everyone's attention back to him.

His remark also caused Zeke's eyes to narrow. "Think before you say anything," Zeke warned him.

But Greg didn't even pause. "I saw something at Rocky Creek that night Webb went missing. Something that made me a target for a killer."

Wyatt got an uneasy feeling in the pit of his stomach. "What'd you see?"

Greg swallowed hard. "The person who helped kill Jonah Webb."

Chapter Eleven

A dozen questions went through Lyla's mind, but first and foremost—was Greg telling the truth? And if so, why was he coming clean now? Still, those were questions that might have to wait to be answered because of the last bombshell that Greg had just dropped.

"Well?" Travis snapped. "Spill it. Who'd you see? And if that lie comes out of your mouth saying it was me, you'll regret it."

Greg ignored the threat and looked at Wyatt. "It was Kirby."

Wyatt started cursing, and because she wasn't sure what he was going to do, Lyla put her hand on his arm to try to steady him.

"You didn't see Kirby kill Webb because he didn't do it," Wyatt insisted.

"I didn't see him put the knife in Webb," Greg explained, "but I did see him leave Webb's office that night."

Wyatt cursed some more. "Kirby could have been there for a variety of reasons. Webb had beaten up Declan that day. He'd hit one of the girls, too."

Both good reasons for Kirby to have paid a visit to the headmaster, but obviously he hadn't told Wyatt about it.

"What exactly did you see?" Lyla asked Greg. And

she tried to make note of not just his body language but Travis and Zeke's. That might help her figure out what was really going on here.

"I was in the storage closet just down the hall from Webb's office." Greg's voice was low and strained. He glanced at the floor. At her. Even at Wyatt and Travis. At everyone but his mentor, Zeke. "I used to go there sometimes when I wanted to be alone."

"Go ahead," Zeke pressed when Greg paused. "You opened this can of worms, and it's too late to stop now. Tell them *everything*."

And either Zeke was acting, or else he truly hadn't wanted this to come to light. But she couldn't imagine why. Because if Greg was telling the truth, this took the blame off everyone else, including Zeke, and put it on Kirby.

Greg bobbed his head but still didn't look at Zeke. "I heard someone arguing in Webb's office. A lot of arguing," he corrected. "First, with Stella. She was upset about the way Webb had hit Declan." His gaze came to Wyatt's. "Webb slapped her."

Because she still had hold of his arm, she felt Wyatt's muscles turn to iron, and it took a while to get his teeth unclenched. "You should have come and told me."

"And me," Harlan added.

"You both would have killed him."

Harlan's expression took on a dangerous edge that matched Wyatt's. "Damn right."

Greg shook his head. "I was only sixteen, but I wasn't stupid. I could see what was going on, and I knew it could turn deadly if the wrong people found out what Webb had done to her. Anyway, Stella and he argued for a while, and then she stormed out."

"And Webb was alive when she left?" Lyla pressed.

"Oh, yes. He got other visitors after her." He paused again. "Zeke came."

Travis's face lit up, and he made a sound to indicate this wasn't a surprise to him. "This just keeps getting better and better."

"I already told the sheriff and the Rangers that I was there that night," Zeke readily admitted. "Webb and I were friends, and he called me after his little run-in with Stella. She'd told him she was reporting him to the state officials, and I tried to calm him down so he wouldn't do something he'd regret. Like fire her. Because that would have only made her go after him even harder."

Lyla figured this was difficult for Wyatt to hear. Stella was like a mother to him, and she had put herself in danger by going up against Webb like that.

"Stella never told you about this run-in with Webb?" she whispered to Wyatt.

His jaw muscles stirred again, and he shook his head. "That doesn't mean she's guilty."

No, it didn't, but Lyla did have to wonder why she'd kept it secret all these years. Of course, maybe Stella hadn't wanted to add any more horrible memories to the ones that her *boys* already had.

"After Zeke left Webb's office," Greg continued, "Sarah went into the room. A few minutes later, Kirby arrived. They argued, too. I couldn't hear about what exactly, but their voices were raised. And then everything got quiet. Kirby left, and he shut the door behind him. Sarah stayed inside, but I don't have any idea when she came out, because I fell asleep."

"That doesn't mean Kirby helped kill him." Wyatt scrubbed his hand over his face. "Besides, the blood spatter found at Rocky Creek points to the initial attack happening in Stella's quarters."

Greg shook his head again. "I'm not sure why that blood was there. I'm just telling you what I saw and heard. And because of it, someone tried to kill me."

"What you *saw and heard* doesn't make sense," Wyatt snarled. "If Kirby didn't know you were in that closet, then how would he have known to *silence* you?"

"Maybe you should ask Kirby." Greg checked his watch. "He should be here any minute."

"What?" Wyatt snapped. "Why would Kirby come here?" And now it was Wyatt's eyes that took on a dangerous edge.

Harlan's, too. He grabbed his phone. No doubt to call the ranch.

"I called Kirby," Greg explained. "Told him I was coming here and told him what I was going to say."

"That you were going to accuse him of murder," Wyatt snapped, and he looked at Harlan, who only nodded.

"Kirby's on the way," Harlan verified. "And Stella didn't know. Now she's on the way, too."

"Well, well," Travis mocked. "Soon the whole gang will be here, and this is one show I don't want to miss."

Wyatt gave him a glare that could have withered every blade of grass in Texas. "Who's with Kirby?" he asked his brother. "And can you stop him from coming?"

"Cutter's bringing him, and they're already in the parking lot."

"Cutter?" she whispered to Wyatt.

"He's a ranch hand," Wyatt explained.

And that in itself told her that Kirby had sneaked away not just from Stella but the rest of the family, as well. Probably because he knew they would have stopped him.

But why was he coming?

Hopefully to explain the accusation Greg had just made. Of course, it wasn't so much an accusation. More of an observation, and it certainly didn't prove Kirby was a killer. So, why had he felt the need to come here? Apparently, they wouldn't have to wait long for that answer.

"Excuse us for a second," Lyla said, and despite Wyatt's attempts to stay put, she led him into Saul's office. She didn't shut the door, but she maneuvered him to the other side of the room so they wouldn't be heard.

"I won't let them railroad Kirby." And he tried to get around her. But Lyla held on, pinning him against the wall. Of course, he could have thrown off her grip at any time, but he didn't. He continued to curse and mumble for several more seconds before he stilled and looked at her.

"Kirby's getting better, but he's still weak from the cancer treatments," Wyatt said. "We came close to losing him."

Lyla heard the emotion in his voice. Saw it more in his eyes, and she slid her arms around him and pulled him to her. "I'm sorry for all of you."

"For us," he corrected. Still looking as if he wanted to battle something, anything, he brushed a kiss on her forehead. "You're caught in the middle of this, too. You and the baby."

But then the intense warrior look changed. Maybe because of the baby. He was no doubt still coming to terms with the fact that the child was his.

Lyla was certainly struggling with it.

Wyatt gently pushed away a strand of her ponytail that had slipped onto her neck. The back of his fingers brushed against her skin. And just like that, she got the jolt of heat.

So did he.

Because he kissed her again.

This time on her mouth, and he lingered a bit, adding more and more to that heat. Maybe because he wanted to escape for just a few moments. Lyla understood that. She was escaping, too, except it felt like a lot more than that.

He slid his hand between them. Over her belly. "I don't want any of this to hurt you."

She was pretty sure he wasn't just talking about the danger now. Or just the situation they had to work out with the baby. But it was already too late for avoiding hurt. She was well on her way to getting her heart crushed.

Again.

Apparently, she hadn't learned anything when it came to love.

"Kirby's coming into the building," Harlan called out.

Wyatt didn't rush out, and she looked up at him, dreading what she had to ask. "Did Kirby help kill Webb?"

His mouth tightened, the response he usually had when anyone questioned Kirby's innocence, but then he shook his head. "I honestly don't know. In fact, the only person in my family that I'm positive is innocent is me."

That was what she was afraid he was going to say, and that could mean this meeting with Kirby could have devastating consequence. Because she doubted any of their other suspects were on the verge of a confession. They were still too busy blaming each other.

She followed Wyatt back into the squad room, and he went into the hall to wait by the elevator near the stairs. No doubt where Kirby would be making his arrival. But even though they had only a few moments, Lyla decided to keep digging for information that Greg might or might not have.

"That night when you were in the storage closet, did you hear a noise, like a body falling to the floor?" she asked the man. "Because it would have made a heavy, thudding sound." And if he'd been able to hear voices as he'd claimed, he wouldn't have missed that sound.

"I heard some things. Maybe not a thud exactly, but more like someone moving furniture or something."

So, maybe after being stabbed, Webb had fallen onto a chair or some other piece of furniture. Without Sarah alive to tell them, they might never know. Well, unless they got a confession from her accomplice.

Or her killer.

Of course, that could be the same person, but clearly Wyatt didn't believe it was his foster father.

"You shouldn't have come here," Wyatt immediately said when Kirby rolled into the room in his wheelchair. "And you shouldn't have brought him," he added to the ranch hand who stayed in the hall.

"When I saw him gettin' into his truck, or rather tryin' to do that, he told me he'd drive here on his own if I didn't bring him," Cutter protested.

"And I would have," Kirby insisted. "I'm not an invalid, and I can speak for myself." His gaze softened a little when he looked at Harlan, Wyatt and her, but there was no soft look for Greg. "Greg, aka Spenser Cash, called and said he was about to implicate me in Webb's murder. As far as I was concerned, that was throwing down the gauntlet."

"A gauntlet you should have let Wyatt and me pick up," Harlan insisted.

Kirby shook his head. "Like I said, I'm not an invalid, and I wasn't going to sit by at the ranch while Greg spins a web of lies."

"No lies. I was just telling them what I saw and heard," Greg argued. "I'm sorry if that points to you being Sarah's accomplice."

"I doubt you're sorry," Wyatt snapped. "And you're

just spilling all of this now?" He didn't wait for an answer. "Why didn't you speak up all those years ago?"

"Because he was a scared kid," Zeke said.

Wyatt shot him a *back off* glare. "I'd like to hear it from him."

Greg took a moment, gathering his breath. "Because I wasn't sorry that Webb was gone. I didn't know he was dead. I just knew he wasn't around to beat us anymore, and I didn't really care who was responsible for that." He paused. "Well, not until the threats started."

"What threats?" Lyla asked. Again, she watched the body language. Travis was enjoying this far too much, but he was the only one.

"They started within days after Webb disappeared," Greg continued. "Notes telling me to stay quiet about what I saw. The notes escalated to the tires on my foster parents' car being slashed."

"That's when I stepped in," Zeke explained. "I told him he'd never be safe if he didn't disappear, too. I helped him get a new identity, and eventually we started a business together."

"You withheld information pertinent to a murder investigation," Lyla accused.

That earned her a hard look from the retired sheriff. "I didn't know Webb had been murdered then. Thought he'd just walked out on Sarah and turned his back on Rocky Creek. I didn't know he was dead until his body was found eight months ago."

"Right," Travis snarled. "He was your so-called friend, and you didn't think it strange that he hadn't contacted you in nearly seventeen years?"

Zeke turned that frosty look on Travis. "One breath you accuse me of wrongdoing. The next, it's Kirby or Greg. The only person you're not accusing is yourself."

Travis smiled. "Because I wasn't there that night that someone put a knife in Webb's ribs. Unlike others." His gaze landed on Kirby. "So, are you here to confess, Marshal?"

"No," someone said.

Everyone turned in the direction of the doorway, to find Stella standing there. She was breathing hard, probably because she'd run to get into the building.

"Kirby's not here to confess," Stella insisted. Her narrowed gaze landed on Travis. "But I am."

The room went totally silent, but it was the calm before the storm. Wyatt went toward her, but Kirby was closer, and he whirled his chair around to face her.

"You're not doing this," Kirby insisted, and both Harlan and Wyatt echoed the same. "You're not lying to protect me."

Stella lifted her chin. "Not to protect you. And I'm not lying, because it's true." Her determined gaze came to Wyatt. "You need to arrest me because I'm the one who helped Sarah kill her husband."

Chapter Twelve

The day was still going at breakneck speed, but one look at Lyla, and Wyatt knew he had to slow down this pace. At least temporarily so he could get her back to the ranch.

She was literally asleep at his desk.

Worse, Wyatt wasn't sure how long she'd been that way. He'd gotten so caught up in trying to help Stella and dealing with the investigation that he hadn't realized just how late it was. Half past three, which meant she'd spent the better part of the day at the marshals' building. Considering she'd slept very little the night before, she had to be exhausted, and that wasn't good for either her or the baby.

"I'm getting Lyla out of here," he told Declan. Like Wyatt, his brother had been on the phone for hours, still was, but he gave Wyatt a go-ahead nod.

Leaving didn't mean Wyatt wouldn't continue to help. All of his brothers had pitched in to try to stop Stella's arrest, but so far they were batting zero. Mainly because Stella wasn't cooperating. She'd lawyered up and was refusing to talk to any of them.

That didn't make her guilty.

Well, guilty of murder anyway. No. She was almost certainly doing this to protect Kirby. Unfortunately, Greg's statement, which he'd now officially made and signed, put Stella at the crime scene, and that slap from Webb gave her a motive.

"How about you?" Wyatt asked Kirby. "Want a ride back with us?"

But he knew Kirby's answer before he'd even asked the question. Kirby just shook his head.

On a weary huff, Wyatt grabbed their coats, went to his desk and gave Lyla a gentle tap on the shoulder. She snapped to a sitting position, but then she looked around as if trying to figure out where she was.

"Oh, sorry," she mumbled. "I didn't mean to fall asleep." She yawned and rubbed her eyes.

"Don't be. You needed the rest, and I should have gotten you home by now. To the ranch," he corrected when he realized what he'd said.

It wasn't Lyla's home, and he was reasonably sure she didn't want to be there. But that didn't matter. He wasn't letting her out of his sight.

She stood, wobbling a little, and he resisted the urge to scoop her up into his arms and carry her down the stairs. Four of his brothers were in the office. And his boss. Along with Kirby, who was refusing to leave. Best not to have to explain to his family yet why he'd be carrying a perfectly healthy woman. But he'd have to explain things soon.

Once they had Stella's confession nixed.

Lyla glanced around the room as they put on their coats and headed out. "Please tell me that Travis, Zeke and Greg haven't all been released."

"Travis has. No grounds to hold him, since we still haven't made a concrete connection between him and the missing gunman. Greg's in the interview room, finishing up his statement with Ranger McKinnon, and Zeke's in another room, waiting his turn to be interviewed."

"And Stella?" she asked hesitantly.

"In Saul's office with her lawyer. Unless something drastic happens, Ranger McKinnon will take her into custody when he's finished with Zeke."

That sounded about as unright as anything could sound. Stella was going to be placed under arrest, and so far there was nothing he could do to stop it.

Wyatt paused at the front door, looked out. He half expected Travis to be there, waiting to add some wise-cracking remark that would make Wyatt want to break his face. But no Travis. No sign of a gunman, either. So, Wyatt got her moving to his SUV.

The clouds were iron-gray, and the temperature had dropped. There'd been no time to check the weather, but it looked as if a winter storm was moving in. The way his luck had been running, they'd get a blizzard.

"What else did I miss when I was asleep?" she asked once they were on the road.

A lot. But Wyatt wouldn't tell her about the family debate on how to handle Stella's confession. It hadn't been pretty and had involved a lot of emotion. All of them had agreed to try to have the confession tossed out, but none of them had come up with a reasonable way to make that happen.

Though some unreasonable ways had been bantered about.

Kirby had wanted to hog-tie her.

No need to go through all of that again, so Wyatt stuck to the investigation itself.

"It was rattlesnake venom used to kill Sarah," he explained. "But it's a dead end because it was such a small amount that the killer could have gotten it from dozens of places around the state."

She groaned softly, obviously disappointed about that.

"What about the surveillance footage? Anyone other than Greg and Zeke on it? Or should I say Spenser and Zeke?"

She said Spenser's name as if it were profanity. Wyatt felt the same way. He sure as hell didn't like that the man had waltzed in after all these years and implicated Kirby.

Which was probably the reason Stella had confessed.

"Neither Travis nor Billy popped up on the footage." But Wyatt had to shake his head. "Of course, they could have come in earlier and just waited around."

"Or they could have just hired someone," she added. "Someone whose face wouldn't have stuck out on the security cameras."

Yeah. And that, too, was something that Wyatt had already considered. But it didn't rule out any of their suspects. Even Greg and Zeke. Because one of them could be behind this and still have shown up at the hospital to make himself look as if he'd been set up.

"There was a landline in Sarah's room," Wyatt continued, "and it was off the hook, as if someone had just used it."

"You mean Sarah?"

Wyatt lifted a shoulder and made another check of the mirrors. No one else was on the road. "Her prints are on it."

"That's not proof. The prints could have been planted there by simply taking her hand and putting it on the surface. But if I could take a look at it, I might be able to determine pressure points. If someone was holding her hand on that phone, sometimes the grip pattern is off."

"Giving you access to the evidence might be hard to do." He figured that would get her looking in his direction, and it did.

"I'm officially off the case?"

He nodded. "The governor's assistant called and made

it clear that we weren't to have any part of this. But that doesn't mean we can't continue to investigate on our own. Maybe after you get something to eat, then you can call one of your CSI friends who can in turn contact the lab and make sure they're doing a check for the grip pattern on the phone."

"Of course." He heard the disappointment in her voice. They'd known they would be taken off the case, but it felt like being fired for doing something wrong. Well, he'd done wrong, all right, but it'd been for the right reasons.

To keep Lyla safe.

And if necessary, he'd continue to do wrong.

"I spoke with Sarah's doctor," Wyatt went on, "and he said she had been responding more lately and that he thought she might be coming out of the coma."

"Billy was right," she mumbled.

About that anyway. But since this whole mess with Greg, Zeke and Travis, Wyatt wasn't ready to completely eliminate Billy as a suspect in either his father or his mother's murders.

Lyla stayed quiet a moment, obviously giving that some thought. "Is it possible that Sarah came out of the coma but then pretended to still be in one?"

"It's possible." Wyatt had asked the doctor that, too. And if that's what had indeed happened, then she could have made the calls herself.

But why?

Could Sarah have done that to get her accomplice to come to her room, or had she made the calls because she'd been genuinely afraid for her life? Unfortunately, the answer to that might be buried with her.

Wyatt took the final turn toward the ranch when he heard the sound. A loud popping noise. The steering wheel immediately jolted to the right, followed by a much louder sound as if a helicopter were hovering overhead.

No helicopter though.

"The tire blew out," he told Lyla.

Not the best time for something like this to happen, but at least they were close to the ranch. The white fence surrounding the pasture was just ahead and to his right. Rather than take the time to change the tire himself and risk being out in the open with Lyla, he could just call one of the ranch hands to come and get them.

Lyla grabbed on to the dash. Just in time. Because there was another hard turn of the steering wheel, followed by the grinding noise of his tire rims scraping over the asphalt. He had no choice but to bring the SUV to a stop on the shoulder.

Everything inside Wyatt went still.

What were the odds that he'd have two blowouts within seconds of each other when he hadn't seen any debris on the road?

Slim to none.

"Get down!" he ordered Lyla.

But his warning was already too late. The bullet blasted across the top of the SUV.

LYLA DIDN'T HAVE TIME to react. But Wyatt sure did. He shoved her down on the seat, covering her body with his, and in the same motion, he drew his gun.

Just as another shot slammed into the SUV.

The fear was instant. So was the burst of adrenaline. Followed by the absolute terror that her baby and Wyatt could be harmed. They had to get out of there because the bullets just kept coming.

Despite the panic crawling through her, Wyatt seemed

to stay calm, though every muscle in his body had turned to iron. Still, he grabbed his phone and made a call.

"Get someone out here to the east corner of the ranch," he said to whoever answered. "Someone's firing shots at us, and we're pinned down."

That made the fear even worse, but Lyla tried to concentrate on getting out of this deadly situation.

"Did he shoot out all the tires?" Lyla asked.

"I don't think so. But the front two tires are both flat. I think it was some kind of explosive device."

Mercy. That meant this wasn't just some loosely planned attack on a rural road. The device had likely been set earlier. Maybe even while they were in the marshals' building. Of course, there'd been plenty of opportunity, since they'd been there for hours. It could have happened when she'd fallen asleep, and Lyla cursed herself for that lapse in attention.

"I should have kept watch when we were in town," she mumbled.

"Whoever's behind this would have found a way to make an attack happen," he mumbled right back.

That was no doubt true, but knowing the truth didn't make this situation less dangerous. Why had the killer come after them now and like this? The blood evidence at Rocky Creek had been destroyed, and Stella had confessed to being Sarah's accomplice. Not that she'd actually done it, but why would that matter to the real killer?

Unless there was something else out there that needed to be concealed or destroyed.

Still, that didn't answer her question as to why someone had come after Wyatt and her again.

"The shooter's on the driver's side," Wyatt told her. "Probably in those woods, and he's using a rifle. But I don't think he wants us dead. If he did, he could have set a bigger explosive device on the SUV."

True, and that only caused her heart to race even more. "So, this is a kidnapping attempt?"

"Maybe. Or maybe he only wants you alive."

So he could force her to tamper with evidence. Except, that didn't make sense, since she was officially off the case. Unless this person believed she'd still have access to the evidence.

And she probably could get access.

But not without compromising the entire investigation.

Which might be exactly what the killer wanted to happen. After all, it wasn't just one murder now. With Sarah's death, it was two.

"Hold on," Wyatt told her, and that was the only warning she got before he threw the SUV into gear, caught onto the steering wheel with his left hand and hit the accelerator.

The SUV lurched forward, and despite the two flat tires, somehow Wyatt managed to turn them in the direction of the white fence. It was at least eight feet high. Too high to climb with the bullets flying, but if they could somehow manage to get over it, there were some trees on the other side that they could use for cover.

Maybe.

Unless there was someone waiting for them there.

What they needed was backup, and it was no doubt already on the way thanks to Wyatt's call. Lyla wasn't sure how far they were from the ranch, but she thought it was only a mile or two. However, that was way too much, considering they were in the sights of a shooter.

The muscles in Wyatt's face and arms strained to keep the SUV aimed at the fence, and even though he'd told her to stay down, she had to do something to help. She reached around, gripping the steering wheel with him. It was like pulling at dead weight, but they continued toward the fence.

Wyatt didn't hit the brakes as they got closer. The SUV plowed right through it, sending the wooden planks flying and battering into the vehicle. Finally, he brought them to a stop next to a pair of oaks. All in all, it was a good position, because the SUV would block the shooter's view once they were out the passenger's side door.

"Get behind the tree," he insisted. "But stay low and move fast."

Even though her hands were shaking like crazy, Lyla managed to get the door open, and she practically dove out of the SUV. She landed on her feet behind one of the oaks, and she made room for Wyatt so he could join her.

But he didn't do that.

His phone buzzed, and he hit the answer button. Lyla couldn't hear any of his conversation because of the gunfire, but when he finished the call, Wyatt glanced at her.

"Get on the ground and crawl to that next tree," he ordered.

She did, scrambling to put some more distance between the shooter and her.

Wyatt, however, didn't do the same.

"Come on!" she shouted to him.

But Wyatt only shook his head. He took aim at the shooter from the driver's side window and fired.

"Go with him," Wyatt insisted.

It took Lyla a second to figure out what he meant. Then she heard the sound of a horse's gallop and spotted the ranch hand on a pinto.

"Go!" Wyatt repeated.

Lyla shook her head. "Not without you."

Wyatt's gaze met hers. "Think of the baby."

That was playing dirty, but she couldn't ignore the risk to the baby. Even if the shooter somehow managed to kidnap her, heaven knew what would happen to them. And to Wyatt.

"Go ahead," Wyatt added. "I'll be right behind you."

"Move now!" the ranch hand called out to her.

Lyla couldn't take the time to debate this any longer, so she darted through the trees toward the pinto. The moment she reached them, the ranch hand caught her by the arm and levered her onto the back of the saddle before he got the pinto moving.

Fast.

She tried to get one last glimpse of Wyatt, but the hand immediately maneuvered them into yet another group of trees. Away from the danger.

Away from Wyatt.

And even over the sound of her heartbeat crashing in her ears, Lyla heard the shots slam nonstop into the SUV.

Chapter Thirteen

Wyatt sent another shot in the direction of the gunman, who was obviously trying to kill him. But at least Lyla was out of harm's way.

For now.

The ranch hand, John Busby, had worked on the ranch for years and was someone Wyatt trusted. Busby would get her back to the house and guard her until Wyatt managed to join them. And when Wyatt's phone buzzed again, he hoped it was news that would speed up his doing just that.

"Almost there," Declan greeted him. "Dallas, too. He's coming from the other direction. He didn't want to leave until he made sure the others were locked in and safe."

Wyatt couldn't blame him. Both Caitlyn and Joelle were pregnant, too, and plus, Slade's and Clayton's infant sons were there. That was a lot of people who had to be protected on the ranch. Normally, the doors wouldn't be locked, but they would be until the danger had passed.

The second that Wyatt pushed the end-call button, he heard the sirens. Declan, no doubt. And his brother's loud approach got the results Wyatt needed.

The gunman stopped firing.

Wyatt immediately grabbed his phone and called Dallas. "The shooter's getting away. Get someone to that old ranch road on the west. That's probably his escape route."

"Will do," Dallas assured him. "Now get back to the main house. Lyla's worried about you."

That worry had to be pretty extreme for Dallas to even mention it, so the moment Declan pulled to a stop on the road, Wyatt kept low but made his way to the truck. Declan didn't waste any time getting them out of there.

"You okay?" Declan asked.

Wyatt nodded, but he was far from okay. "How was Busby so close to us when the shooting started?"

"He was out riding fence, and I had Cutter call him."

So, they'd gotten lucky. Wyatt hated that it'd taken something as random as luck to keep Lyla and the baby from being hurt. Or worse.

"I think someone was trying to kidnap Lyla," Wyatt told his brother.

Declan cursed, pushed the accelerator even harder and sped toward the ranch. Busby was on the porch, his rifle ready and aimed, and Wyatt spotted Lyla in the window. Despite Busby yelling for her to stay inside, she threw open the front door, barreled down the steps and landed right in Wyatt's arms.

It didn't feel like a hug from a fake wife. Neither did the kiss she planted on his mouth. Or the tears that were in her eyes. Those were caused by genuine worry and fear. Of course, it didn't mean her reaction was more than that. And Wyatt didn't want it to be. However, it gave him some reassurance, too, to have her in his arms.

"You weren't hurt?" she asked, her voice trembling.

"No." And Wyatt got her moving back toward the door, because he didn't want her out in the open with the rifleman on the loose. He looked at Busby. "Come in and stand guard. I want someone else watching the back of the house."

Busby nodded, took out his phone and followed them in.

"I'll help Dallas look for this guy," Declan offered. "But everybody should stay inside with the doors locked."

Wyatt did exactly that, and he set the security system once he had Lyla and Busby in the foyer. He didn't arm the security just for the house but for the sensors that were scattered over the property. It didn't mean someone couldn't get through, but at least they'd have a warning if that happened.

"Busby said no one else is here," Lyla told him. "They're all at Dallas and Joelle's house."

"I brought her here because it was closer," Busby explained.

A wise decision.

"Thanks for getting Lyla out of there," he told the man.

Busby just nodded. "You think the shooter's coming back for another round?"

"I think we're okay for now." But it was a lie. Wyatt had no idea what would happen other than he would do whatever it took to keep Lyla safe.

"Grab a chair from the den if you want," Wyatt offered the man. "You might be here a while. And once the other ranch hand's here to guard the back, let him in, but then make sure the security system is reset."

"Will do. I'll give a yell if I see or hear anything."

And Wyatt would do the same. Once he had Lyla settled.

But he debated where to take her. There were too many windows in the kitchen and the den.

In most rooms, actually.

Plus, she was shaking all over now and likely ready to crash. But he still needed to be where he could monitor the security sensors and camera. So, he led her toward the ranch's main office on the side of the house. Too bad he couldn't offer her some whiskey to settle her nerves, because she was going to need something.

The room was much larger than his own office, and while it wouldn't be as comfortable as one of the bedrooms, it'd have to do. Keeping an eye on her, Wyatt booted up the laptop on the desk that Kirby had used daily before he got sick. These days, it fell mainly to Wyatt and his brothers.

"People keep shooting at us," Lyla said under her breath.

Wyatt considered a bullet-magnet joke, but the fear was still too fresh and too raw for that. He had her sit on the leather sofa, and even though it wouldn't do much in the nerve-steadying department, he handed her a bottle of water.

"You need to see a doctor?" he asked, praying that she didn't. It might not be safe to get a doctor out here with a gunman on the loose. Still, he'd make it happen if she needed medical attention.

But she didn't answer. Lyla took the plastic bottle of water as if it were fragile and might crack in her hand, and she set it aside on the table. With that same level of fragility, she stood and buried her face against his shoulder.

"We can't keep going through this." Her breath broke, and Wyatt braced himself for the tears to start. But there were no tears in her eyes when she pulled back and met his gaze.

"I want to get this bastard," she said. "I want to stop him before he hurts us."

Wyatt wanted the same, with another demand tacked on to hers. He wanted to make this jerk pay for putting Lyla through another ordeal.

She eased back even farther, looking a little stronger now, and tipped her head to the laptop. "We need to watch to make sure the gunman doesn't try to get on the ranch."

"If anyone comes across the fence or the road, it'll trigger a sensor that'll give us a warning beep." But just in case the shooter figured out some way to jam that specific sensor, Wyatt turned the laptop in the direction of the sofa. The security system had cameras so even if they lost the warning sensor, they should still be able to see what was going on. He had Lyla sit again so she could watch.

But she didn't sit by herself.

She caught onto his hand and pulled him down beside her.

"I can't imagine going through this alone," she whispered.

He heard every ounce of raw emotion in that. Saw it in her eyes, too. And silently cursing the gunman and the person who'd hired him, Wyatt put his arm around her and drew her closer.

Lyla looked up at him. "This is a mistake. I'm sure of it."

Wyatt had to shake his head because he wasn't sure what she meant.

Until she kissed him.

But she didn't just *kiss* him. She coiled her arms around him, put her mouth on his and kissed him the right way. Well, the right way if this had been a real make-out session and not just some reaction to the shooting. Everything else about it was wrong, especially the timing.

"You could cost me everything," she said with her mouth against his.

She was talking about the baby now, something Wyatt wasn't sure they should discuss. Not with too many other things unsettled. But the one thing that was settled was this blasted attraction between them.

It was getting stronger with each passing second.

Of course, that kiss sure as heck hadn't helped.

Neither would what he was about to do. He was about to take one wrong kiss and turn it into an even bigger one. One that he was certain they'd regret, but even knowing that didn't stop him.

Cursing himself and cursing her, Wyatt latched on to the back of her hair, not gently, either, and he hauled her even closer until they were tangled against each other. The kiss continued. Raging like the fire building inside him. Man, he wanted her.

And he did something about that.

He pulled her onto his lap so he could kiss her neck. And so he could kiss lower, too. He was still too rough and tried to slow down. Tried to take things easier. But Lyla clearly wanted no part of easier, because she pulled him right back to her when he tried to ease away.

She was wearing a stretchy sweater top, and with one tug he shoved it up and had access to the tops of her breasts. He kissed her there. First one, then the other. And his own body reacted to the breathy little moan of pleasure she made deep in her throat.

So, Wyatt ignored the big warning in his head and pretty much gave in to what a different part of him was demanding. Of course, that part often came up with stupid demands, but he'd already crossed so many lines with Lyla that it didn't take much to keep crossing more.

He shoved down her bra, and her breasts spilled into his hands. Oh, man. She was perfect.

And he was toast.

He didn't stop. Wyatt kept touching her. Kept kissing her. Until the ache inside was well past the point of no return.

"I can't catch my breath," she said, and went after his mouth again.

Great. She was acting just as reckless as he was, and Wyatt had counted on her to stop this.

It had to stop.

But it took him several moments to remember why exactly that had to be. And the reason was his wife, Ann. Except, Lyla was his wife now.

In name only.

Of course, they were blowing that big-time. If these kisses and touches kept up, this marriage would be consummated the old-fashioned way. With a great round of sex.

And he was sure it would be great.

With this much fire and energy between them, there was no chance it would be bad, which meant once they'd finished this mistake, he would almost certainly want to make another one with her.

Lyla stopped so she could drag in some air, and when she came back with one of those deep, mind-blowing kisses, she turned, easing back onto the sofa and pulling him down with her.

Or, rather, on top of her.

Probably the worst place for him to be, but Wyatt went there anyway until he knew the next step would involve clothing removal.

And it would have if not for the buzzing sound.

Because he had only one thing on his mind—sex with Lyla—it took him a moment to realize it was a phone.

Hell. This could be critical. There was a gunman on the loose near the ranch, and Wyatt had gotten so caught up with Lyla that he'd forgotten everything that he sure as heck should be remembering.

"Hold that thought," he told Lyla, moving her hand from his zipper. Though he should have been telling her to forget all about it. Not that he could do that, but maybe she'd see this from a different angle.

The right one.

He got up. Not easily. He could barely stand, because he was hard as stone. And he looked at the name on the phone screen. Not one of his brothers, thank God, with bad news about the shooter.

It was Billy.

Of course, this could be bad news of a different kind. Lately, no one had been calling him just to chat, and he figured that wasn't happening now.

"I'm sorry," Billy said the moment Wyatt answered.

Wyatt groaned. An apology wasn't a good start to a conversation. "Sorry for what?" And he was certain he wasn't going to like this answer.

"I know why someone just tried to kill you, Wyatt. And it's all my fault."

EVEN THOUGH WYATT didn't have the call on speaker, Lyla could hear what Billy said, and she immediately got to her feet and fixed her clothes. Obviously, the kissing session was finished.

Or at least delayed.

Because it was clear that Billy had something important to tell them.

Lyla motioned for Wyatt to put the call on speaker, and he did, just as Billy's voice poured through the room.

"I wanted to find out who killed my mother," Billy said. "So, I lied. I made some calls and put out the word that she'd kept something from the night my father died. Something she gave me so that it could be analyzed."

"What are you talking about?" Wyatt asked, taking the question right out of Lyla's mouth.

"I lied," he repeated, but that didn't explain anything. "I told some people that I found the tape that my mother had mentioned. I said it was scratchy, very poor quality, but it was a recorded conversation between my mother and the person who helped her kill my father."

Oh, mercy. Lyla's heart started racing. "You said you gave it to me to be analyzed, didn't you?"

"Yes. You were the only person I could think of, because you work with evidence like that and crime scenes. And I told the people I called that I didn't want the Rangers to know the results yet just in case the evidence pointed to someone I wanted to protect. Like one of the kids from Rocky Creek."

Wyatt started cursing. Lyla wanted to do the same, but she couldn't muster the breath.

"Who did you tell, Billy?" Wyatt snapped.

"All of them." He hesitated, mumbled something that she didn't catch. "Kirby, Stella, Zeke, Greg and Travis. I called them and told them one by one. Well, except for Stella, and I told Kirby to tell her, because she didn't answer her phone."

Now Lyla cursed. Billy had put her directly in the path of a kidnapper, at best.

A killer at worst.

Because the accomplice would no doubt do anything

to keep her from detecting his or her voice in what would essentially be a murder confession.

"I thought the person would give us some warning so we could trap him," Billy quickly added. "Or I thought maybe he'd try to work out some kind of deal to get back the tape. I didn't think he'd try to shoot you."

"Well, you thought wrong." Wyatt's voice was a low, dangerous growl, and Lyla thought if he could reach through the phone and grab Billy, he would. That was what she wanted to do.

"I know, and I'm sorry. So sorry. I'm going to try to fix this."

"No—" Wyatt practically shouted, but he was already too late. Billy had ended the call. "He'll get himself killed."

Or get someone else killed—like Wyatt or her. Either way, he had to be stopped.

Wyatt called Declan, and while Lyla paced, he filled his brother in on what Billy had done.

"I'll see what I can do to stop him," Declan promised. "But in the meantime, I've got more bad news. We didn't catch the gunman. I saw him get away. I'm on my way back to the marshals' office now to see what I can do about talking Stella out of this stupid confession."

"I'll come with you."

"No, you won't. Not after what just happened to Lyla. It's not a good idea for you two to be out and about."

Wyatt looked at her, and she saw the debate in his eyes. A very short one. "You're right. But call me the second you find out anything."

He clicked the end-call button but stared at the phone as if he was trying to will someone to call with good news. Lyla wanted that, too. Desperately.

"How could Billy have been so stupid?" she mumbled.

"Desperate people do stupid things." And Wyatt looked at her, probably because Wyatt and she had just gone in a stupid direction with the kissing session.

Except it hadn't felt stupid.

It'd felt right. And comforting. And somehow perfect, even when it was far from it.

"So, what do we do now?" she asked, even though she already knew. There was nothing they could do.

"I can't take you out of this house," he said. A reminder she didn't need. "Declan and the others will find a way to fix this."

She figured that was possibly another lie and almost certainly for her benefit. Maybe it was the renewed fear from Billy's call. Or from the realization that she could do absolutely nothing to stop what he'd already set into motion, that they could only wait and see what would happen.

Heck, maybe it was just hormones.

But despite everything they'd just learned, despite another layer of danger, her body was still humming, not for news, but for Wyatt.

And that made her one sick puppy.

She forced herself to take a deep breath to try to clear her head. It didn't work. But she did manage to put a few steps between Wyatt and herself when she went to the other end of the desk. Distance might help.

Or not.

Lyla groaned because she wasn't sure anything would help at this point.

He looked at her, ducking down so that he forced eye contact. One glimpse at her, and he blinked. "Oh. You really held that thought."

Lyla knew exactly what he meant. He was talking about that scalding-hot making out that'd been going on before Billy's call. She'd not only held it. Lyla was still feeling it.

He lifted his shoulder, but there was nothing casual about the gesture. She could feel the intensity coming off him. "We have time to kill." Then he shook his head. "Except you and I both know this isn't about killing time."

Yes, they did. It was about this attraction that was begging to be satisfied.

She was absolutely positive that she shouldn't consider doing this, but Wyatt and she hadn't acted reasonably since they'd first laid eyes on each other. She went to him, ready to kiss him again, but he beat her to it.

Wyatt slid his hand around her, hauled her closer and brought his mouth to hers.

Even though he'd kissed her only moments earlier, this was different. The heat was there. That was a given. It was always there. Along with the need clawing away inside her. She'd given up trying to figure out why she was so attracted to him. Why she let her need for him override common sense, her past.

Override everything.

And Lyla let herself melt against him.

The kiss didn't stay on her mouth. He dropped that heat to her neck. And it didn't stay simple, either. Everything felt as if it were spinning out of control, and the only thing Lyla could do was hold on to Wyatt and let him take her.

"You know we shouldn't be doing this," he said a split second before his hand went underneath her top. He touched her breasts, causing the fire to roar even hotter.

His gaze met hers, maybe to give her a moment to back away again from this. But they were past the point of no return, and Lyla maneuvered him not away from her, but back toward the sofa. Along the way, Wyatt had the good sense to lock the door. Something she hadn't even considered. Again, this wasn't a situation involving reason or logic.

Still kissing, still touching, they landed on the sofa.

Lyla felt the cool leather surface against her bare skin and realized that Wyatt had already shoved up her sweater. But he didn't stop there. He pulled it off, dropped it to the floor and kissed her breasts through her bra.

The heat soared.

And the bra didn't last long, either. He quickly rid her of that and went after the zipper on her jeans. Lyla tried to help him, but she got caught in some kissing and touching of her own. The man tasted as good as he looked. Not just his mouth, either, but his neck, and she figured the rest of him would be equally nice to sample.

Too bad they were already past the foreplay, the sampling stage. Probably because they'd been skirting around this since they'd first met. Not love at first sight. But definitely lust.

Everything was frantic now. The need pushing them to finish this, and Lyla did her own share of pushing them to that finish. Somehow, even though she was dealing with the effects of his clever mouth on her breasts, she managed to get his shirt unbuttoned. He was already so many steps ahead of her, and she wanted to catch up.

She wanted to seduce him as much as he was seducing her.

But she was doomed to fail. Obviously, Wyatt was a lot better at this than she was, and before Lyla managed to locate his zipper, he was already shimmying her shoes and jeans off her.

"You have on too many clothes," she said through her rough breathing.

She did something about that. She shoved his shirt off him and then his jeans. Stripped off his boxers, too. And Lyla got one of those *wow* moments. She'd known that Wyatt looked amazing, of course. Everything about him was past the hot stage, but she realized he was hers.

Well, for this moment anyway.

He couldn't be more than that, but for now, this was enough. It had to be.

"What?" he asked, looking down at her.

Since he seemed to be in tune to everything happening in her body, he'd probably felt the hesitation. But it wasn't a hesitation at all. "I'm just admiring the view."

The corner of his mouth lifted with a smile that only heightened the heat, and his gaze skimmed along her body. All of it. "Yeah, my view's pretty damn good, too."

That just about stole the rest of her breath. As did his next kiss. It wasn't a no-nonsense kind of kiss but one that signaled to her body that this was happening *now*.

He adjusted their positions again, catching onto the back of her knee and anchoring her leg against the outside of his hip. There wasn't much room to maneuver on the sofa, but Lyla forgot all about that when he pushed inside her.

The pleasure exploded in her head.

And through the rest of her.

She gasped. Definitely not in pain. From the pure pleasure. But Wyatt's gaze met hers again. Obviously checking. She assured him that all was perfect by pulling him down to her for a deep kiss.

Everything was deep, too. The way he moved inside her. The grip he had on her leg and the back of her neck.

Lyla wanted it to last, but she knew that wasn't possible. Something burning this hot couldn't last.

She felt the climax ripple through her and tried to hang on to every moment, every sensation. But the pleasure took over, consuming her until there was only one thought, just one word, repeating in her head.

Wyatt. Wyatt. Wyatt.

Chapter Fourteen

Wyatt felt the jolt go through his body. The release that made him mindless, numb and satisfied all at the same time. It was a good way to finish what that kissing session had started.

He buried his face against Lyla's neck. Drew in her scent. And let that and the other sensations slide through him. The feel of her bare skin against his. The soft rhythm of her breath.

Those little aftershocks from her climax that kept gripping on to him.

Yeah, that was a good sensation, all right, and a nudge to his body that it would be ready to take her again soon.

But *soon* was going to have to wait.

He would have preferred to stay there with her arms around him, still deep inside her, but with everything going on, it wasn't a good idea to lie around naked.

Of course, it hadn't been a good idea to have sex with Lyla, either, but that hadn't stopped him. Before he could talk himself out of it, he groaned and started to move off her.

But Lyla slid her leg over his and held him in place. Not that he fought her hard. He was a more than willing captive.

"What, regrets already?" she asked. "I thought it'd

take at least five minutes or so before the panic started to set in."

"Not panic." Because her mouth was so close and she smelled like every good thing rolled into one, he brushed a kiss on her lips.

"But regret," she clarified.

"Some." He hadn't meant to admit that and spoil the moment, but Lyla seemed to be clued in to what was going on his head. "But probably not nearly enough. For what it's worth, I'm sorry that I just complicated the hell out of this."

She lifted her shoulder. "I was an equal participant in the complication." She held the stare a moment longer, and he saw the realization go through her eyes.

Not regret, exactly.

But she had to be mentally playing this out. It would affect everything they did in the future.

Everything.

Now she groaned.

And that was Wyatt's cue to get up and start dressing.

"I didn't even ask you if it was okay for you to have sex," he said, aiming a glance at her stomach.

"Probably because it was hard to ask anything with those French kisses."

He couldn't help it. Wyatt smiled, leaned down and gave her another kiss. "You're being, well, rational about this."

And he wasn't. Especially when his gaze landed on her butt-naked body. Mercy, he wanted her all over again, and he'd just had her. What the heck was wrong with him?

"On the outside I'm being rational," Lyla started. "Inside…"

Wyatt put on his boxers, stared at her, waiting for her

to finish. But she didn't. "You're panicking?" he finished for her.

But she shook her head. "Not exactly. I think I'm feeling panicky because I'm not panicking. That doesn't make sense, I know."

Yeah, it did. Too much about this had felt much better than it should have, considering they both had a baggage-filled past. And then there was the baby.

The ultimate complication.

And yet, it was perfect. Of course, Lyla might dispute that when they sat down to work out custody. Sooner or later, they'd have to do just that.

However, before he could say anything about custody or what'd just happened, his phone buzzed. He had to rifle through the heap of clothes on the floor and locate his jeans and his phone in the pocket. But his heart practically skipped a beat when he saw the name on the screen.

Kirby.

He showed the screen to Lyla, and she immediately got up and started dressing. Like him, she was no doubt bracing herself for more bad news.

"Anything wrong?" Wyatt said the moment he answered, and he put the call on speaker.

"Not with me, but I heard from Declan about the shooting and what Billy did. You and Lyla okay?"

"Yeah." Better than okay. And worse. But Wyatt was going to have to deal with the *worse* later, too. "Billy said he called you and all the other people he considers suspects."

"He did, and it was a stupid thing to do. He could have gotten Lyla and you killed."

Wyatt couldn't argue with that. "I don't think it'll make the killer come after Stella or you. If the killer continues to believe Billy's lie about that tape, then Lyla will remain the target. But take some precautions just in case I'm wrong. Maybe keep Declan or one of the others with you."

"Yes." And that was all Kirby said for several long moments. "Stella's getting out of lockup. For now, I've had her confession suppressed."

Well, that was good news, especially since he hadn't picked up on anything good from Kirby's gloom-and-doom tone. "How'd you manage that?"

"By riling her to the core, that's how. I convinced Saul that she's having some mental issues because of everything going on."

Oh, mercy. Yes, that would have riled her. "But she's coming home?"

"She is. Maybe soon she'll quit glaring and start speaking to me again."

Wyatt actually felt sorry for Kirby, because he knew how much his foster father cared for Stella. But Kirby also cared enough not to see her go to jail for something that she hadn't done.

"Anyway, we'll be on our way back soon," Kirby continued. "Me, Stella and Declan. Dallas, too. He's turned over the hunt for your attacker to the Rangers."

"Smart idea. There's been enough danger for this family." Too bad that danger was just going to continue until they caught the person behind this.

Kirby didn't answer, and that put a tight grip on Wyatt's stomach. "Is something wrong?" Wyatt asked. "Something other than the obvious, I mean?"

"We need to have a family meeting." And with that, Kirby paused a long time. "Call the rest of your brothers and have them come to the main house so they'll be with Lyla and you. I'll bring Billy with me. I've put the ranch hands on alert. All of them are armed and ready in case something goes wrong. I even asked some of them to patrol the fence and road."

That didn't help ease the knot forming in his stomach. "I don't think that's wise to bring Billy here."

"Declan's already disarmed him, and we'll all keep an eye on him."

That still didn't help, since Billy had nearly gotten them killed. "What's this meeting all about?" Wyatt came out and asked.

"It's time," Kirby said, pulling in a weary-sounding breath. "All of you need to know the truth about Jonah Webb's murder."

LYLA STOPPED in the doorway of the family room and studied the crowd that'd gathered. The tension was so thick she could feel it, and it didn't seem to improve when some of Wyatt's family looked at her. Probably because they thought she didn't belong there.

Or maybe it was just because she seemed to be turning into a bullet magnet like Wyatt.

Caitlyn and Joelle offered thin smiles, but the others just couldn't muster it.

Even Stella. Kirby had been right about her glaring, because she was doing it now.

So, maybe this didn't have anything to do with her, but with the possible bad news that was hanging like a dark cloud over the room.

"I can wait upstairs while you have the meeting," Lyla whispered to Wyatt. Not the first offer she'd made. In fact, she'd made several of them shortly after Kirby had called for this family meeting. Emphasis on *family,* and she was pretty sure a fake wife didn't count.

"You should be here," Kirby said, probably because he saw the hesitancy all over her face. "You're right smack-dab in the middle of this mess now, and you should hear what has to be said."

"The baby's in the middle of it, too," Wyatt volunteered. "Yeah, Lyla's pregnant, and it's my baby."

Caitlyn, his brother's pregnant wife, made an *I told you so* sound.

"I don't want her or the baby involved in anything else that's dangerous," Wyatt added.

He probably hadn't meant to make her feel like a gestational carrier. In fact, she was sure he hadn't meant it. But the truth was—it was his baby, not hers. And soon his family would know that, too.

Then how would they react?

Of course, they weren't her biggest worries when it came to this baby. It was Wyatt himself. And now that she'd slept with him, it was going to make their entire situation that much harder.

She heard someone unlocking the front door, and Wyatt eased her behind him. But not before she got a glimpse of the men who came in. Declan and Harlan. Busby, the ranch hand who'd rescued her in the pasture, and he had a firm grip on Billy's arm. He led Billy into the family room.

"Billy's not armed," Declan told everyone. He closed the door, locked it and rearmed the security system.

Billy didn't look exactly happy about being frisked and locked in with a group of people who were riled at him, but Lyla was glad Declan had done it, since Billy might be able to help solve this mess of a puzzle. She was equally glad that Wyatt and all his brothers were wearing their weapons just in case Billy was there to do more than help.

"So, what's this meeting about?" Billy asked.

Lyla wanted to know the same thing. She'd heard what

Kirby had told Wyatt. That they all needed to know the truth about Webb's murder, and that could mean someone in the room was about to make a confession.

Kirby stood. Not easily. Clearly, he was still weak, and he held on to the back of the chair for support. That softened Stella's glare a little, but she didn't get up from the reading chair on the far side of the room. She stayed seated, her gaze fixed on Kirby.

"Since Webb's body was found," Kirby said, "we've all been trying to protect each other. None of you wants Stella and me to go to jail, and we feel the same about you." He looked around the room the way a loving father would.

Until his gaze landed on Billy, that is.

"It's time for the truth," Kirby said to him. "Did you help kill your daddy?"

Billy didn't jump to respond to that, but for several seconds his mouth flattened into a line. "No. And if that's why you brought me here, to try to pin his murder on me, then I'm leaving." He turned to walk out.

"It's not why I asked you here," Kirby insisted. "I just need to get to the truth. I've nearly lost my boys and their wives. Wyatt nearly lost his wife and baby today. This can't go on."

Billy stopped and eased back around. "I didn't help my mother kill him," he finally answered.

Kirby nodded—though it was hard to tell if he believed him—and he looked at Stella. "I won't ask if you did it, because you'd just lie to cover for the rest of us. But you might not need to cover for us. We have to get this out in the open so we can deal with it."

Stella swallowed hard. Nodded. "I didn't help with the murder, but if any one of us is going to jail for it, it'll be me."

"Admirable," Kirby mumbled. "But not very smart. By giving that false confession, it allows the real killer to hide behind it. And the hiding has to end tonight."

It should end with the truth, but Lyla wasn't certain they were anywhere near that point yet. Still, she had some questions that might clear up some things.

"I saw the blood spatter on the wall of your former quarters before the bomb destroyed it," she said to Stella. "There wasn't a lot of blood, but it was something you would have noticed."

Stella gave a weary sigh. "The attack probably did happen there. Or at least I think it could have started there anyway. But I'd moved out of that room earlier in the day because a water pipe had burst and flooded the floor and damaged part of the wall."

Lyla looked at Billy, who confirmed that with a nod. "There was a leak, and Mom told me that Stella had moved rooms." He paused. "But I didn't know if the leak was just an excuse so that no one would see the blood."

"It wasn't an excuse," Stella insisted. "Not on my part anyway. I'd been in the clinic with Declan after Webb had beaten him, so I have no idea what went on in my room. I just know when I tried to get back in, the door was padlocked and my stuff was in the hall."

"And you didn't get suspicious?" Lyla pressed.

"Of course I did. Just hours earlier Webb had beaten my son within an inch of his life. And he'd slapped me when I confronted him about it."

Declan went to his mother, slipped his arm around her shoulders. "It's okay," he murmured to her.

Stella's eyes were filled with tears when she looked at Lyla. "I hoped someone had murdered Webb, and I didn't want to ask questions."

"Because you thought one of us had done it," Declan finished for her. He shook his head. "I didn't kill Webb."

"I didn't, either." Harlan spoke up.

Clayton echoed the same. Then Dallas. Slade, too. Jo-elle and Caitlyn, who'd lived at Rocky Creek at the time of the murders, added their "I didn't" responses.

"I didn't kill him," Wyatt added, "but I'm not sorry he's dead."

And all eyes turned to Kirby.

Lyla hadn't realized she'd been holding her breath until her lungs started to ache, and she forced herself to breathe. Some of the others in the room seemed to have the same trouble—all of them waiting for Kirby to respond.

"I'll confess to the murder," Kirby finally said.

"No, you won't!" Wyatt snapped, but his wasn't the only voice in the room. All his brothers and their wives protested, as well.

"I won't let you sacrifice yourself," Stella insisted. The glare and anger were completely gone from her expression, and she left Declan to go to Kirby's side.

Kirby gave her a flat look. "You were willing to make a false confession for the family."

"Did you kill Webb?" Wyatt demanded. His hands were on his hips now, and his jaw muscles were stirring.

Lyla held her breath again. It seemed everyone in the room did.

Kirby shook his head. "I would have killed him, though, if I could have found him. I went looking for him after I saw what he'd done to Declan, and the bruise on Stella's face. But Webb wasn't anywhere around, and Sarah said she didn't know where he was."

Lyla could practically feel the relief go through every one of them.

"But none of this matters," Kirby continued. "I'm not letting any of you go to jail for killing that piece of scum."

"And you're not going to jail, either." Wyatt's gaze swept around the room. "There's another way. One that'll put the right person behind bars. Yeah, whoever it was did us all a favor by killing Webb, but he's not doing us any favors now. He's trying to kidnap Lyla to force her to falsify evidence."

"Evidence that I faked," Billy mumbled.

"We can use it," Wyatt said. "Because the killer doesn't know it's fake. We can use it to trap him."

"I'm listening," Kirby said. Everyone was. Including Lyla. She was willing to try anything that would get Wyatt, his family and the baby out of harm's way.

"We can leak that we have the tape that Sarah gave Billy. The one with the killer's voice," Wyatt continued. "We can say it's going to a specific crime lab for expedited analysis. And we can make sure the lab is well guarded. When the killer or his henchman shows up, we can arrest him and force a confession."

"Using the fake tape worked before," Billy added. "Well, it worked in the wrong way, because it sent the killer after Lyla, but this time we can leave Lyla completely out of it."

"I have the contacts to leak this," Lyla argued. "I can make it sound official so the killer believes that the recording truly exists and will be tested for voice identification."

Wyatt was shaking his head before she even finished. "You're not getting in the middle of this."

"I don't have to. The killer just has to think that I'm involved. We could arrange for a CSI vehicle to come out here under the guise of picking up the tape."

Wyatt stared at her, obviously processing that, and he finally nodded. "Okay to the CSI pickup and to you making the call to get things started, but no to any involvement on your part after that. We could use the marshals' official communication channels to set up the leak. Maybe the sheriff could even be the one to let it slip."

"I can work on that," Declan volunteered. "I can have Sheriff Geary put in a request for extra security to accompany the tape to a lab, and that's what we can leak."

"What if we say we're transporting the recording to the lab in San Antonio?" Lyla asked. "And that Wyatt and I will be going with the CSIs in the evidence van so we can get the results as soon as they're done?"

"That's good," Declan said. "And I won't create the leak until the van is out here. That way, it won't get attacked en route, and the killer won't have time to plant someone on the vehicle."

A good precaution for the CSIs. But it wouldn't end the danger for Wyatt's brothers and the sheriff. Lyla realized a second too late where this conversation was about to head.

"No," Declan said before Wyatt could speak. "You should stay here with Lyla." His gaze dropped to her stomach. "She's been through enough." He tipped his head to Dallas and Harlan. "You should stay with Caitlyn and Joelle, too."

Slade stood. "I'll do protection detail." His wife, Maya, didn't look pleased about that, but she didn't try to stop him. Maybe she understood this was a risk that the entire family had to take.

"And I'll join you," Declan insisted.

They all looked around as if waiting for someone to bring up a major hitch in this impromptu plan. When no one did, Kirby continued. "Dallas and Harlan should take everyone else to Dallas's house. Everyone except Lyla and Wyatt. That way, they could appear to get into the CSI van, just in case someone has the ranch under long-range surveillance. As backup to the security system, Stella and I can stay here with them and keep watch out the back of the house from my room. They can keep watch out the front."

"That means the CSI van and the route to San Antonio has to be heavily guarded," Wyatt insisted. "And when the van arrives, it can park right next to the house so that no one can tell who's getting inside it."

Again, no one objected, though Stella did look at all of them. "Everyone has to be careful."

And with that, they got moving. Dallas and Harlan started ushering family out. Lyla took out her own phone. She called the lab in San Antonio and requested a pickup for evidence surrendered to her in the Webb murder case.

That would get them moving fast, especially since she'd been removed from the case.

"Bring some security with you," she added, "because it's possible someone might not want this evidence to reach the lab."

Of course, there'd be no such danger until the leak happened, and Declan wouldn't create that until the van had actually arrived.

Everything inside her felt like a huge, tight knot. She'd just made Wyatt and herself bait. His brothers, too. So, this had to work.

But Lyla did think of a potential problem.

A leak of a different kind so that the killer could learn what they were actually going to do.

"Could the killer have hired someone to blend in with the ranch hands or someone else on the grounds?" she asked Wyatt.

"Normally, yes. We don't usually have this high of security, but everyone hired within the past three months
was given paid time off. Like the new horse trainer Dallas had hired and the maid who was sweeping the porch
when I first brought you here."

Yes, she remembered. It was a good precaution to keep
them away just in case they had some kind of connection to the killer. Of course, that didn't mean the killer
hadn't managed to somehow get to a trusted employee.
But Lyla wasn't going to borrow trouble.

Especially since they had enough of it already.

"What now?" she asked Wyatt.

He pulled her to him, brushed a kiss on her forehead.
"We wait."

Chapter Fifteen

Wyatt watched the feed from the security cameras on his laptop and tried not to let Lyla see the hurricane of emotions going on inside him. Declan and Slade were out there, headed toward San Antonio in a CSI van. Maybe on the verge of being ambushed, if this plan turned deadly.

Still, having no plan at all could end up getting them killed, too.

That was why both Dallas and another of the ranch hands were monitoring the feed from the security cameras. Wyatt wasn't only watching the feed, he was also keeping an eye on the front windows in case someone managed to sneak on the ranch. Kirby and Stella were doing the same through the window that faced the backyard.

If something moved out there, they needed to be able to respond immediately. Ditto for anything that could happen to the CSI van. The sheriff and his deputies were following it. Not too closely, though. Because they wanted the killer to make his move.

Which made Slade and Declan bait.

That caused him to feel the rapid pump of his heart.

"You should rest," Lyla suggested again.

But she wasn't taking her own advice. Yes, she was

on the bed while he was at his desk in the corner. And she actually had her head on the pillow, but she'd yet to shut her eyes. Probably wouldn't, either. Because Wyatt figured she had the same worries and doubts he did.

He could have used a drink to steady his nerves but didn't want a cloudy head just in case he had to hurry out to help his brothers. Of course, that would only happen if everything else failed.

Because he couldn't leave Lyla alone.

His other brothers were already tucked away at Dallas's place, and some of the ranch hands were there standing guard. The others were watching the main house and pastures. There was a lot of ground to cover, but Wyatt kept reminding himself that the security system would alert them if anyone tripped any of the sensors. The killer couldn't get onto the ranch without them knowing.

And besides, the highest probability was that the killer would go after that van. To steal the evidence that didn't exist.

Billy had left to go to the sheriff's office in town so he could monitor things from there with the night deputy. It wasn't ideal, especially since Wyatt wasn't sure he could completely trust Billy, but that was the reason he hadn't wanted him to stay at the ranch. There was enough to stretch his attention without adding Billy to the mix.

Outside, the winter wind was slapping at the windows. No snow, but it felt as if it were on the way. Hopefully that didn't mean there'd be ice on the roads. Declan and Slade had enough on their plates without having to deal with Mother Nature.

Wyatt glanced at his phone. No calls yet. Not that he'd expected any. It was too soon to hear from Declan, but *soon* couldn't come soon enough.

"I think Kirby and Stella have resolved their differences," Lyla said. Probably an attempt to make small talk since he no doubt looked ready to come unraveled.

"Yeah. They're in love." Which meant settling differences was a given. He looked at Lyla, at the way she had her hand on her stomach over the baby. "Sometimes, settling differences has to happen even when there isn't love."

That probably wasn't a good thing to toss out there like that, but it was better than small talk. And it was something Lyla and he wouldn't be able to avoid much longer.

Her forehead bunched up, and she eased to a sitting position. "You'll challenge me for custody."

It wasn't a question. And he didn't want to answer it anyway. They needed to discuss this, not start a raging argument.

Since he'd still be able to hear the security system from the bed and glance out the window, Wyatt went closer and sat next to her. She was fully clothed in her jeans and sweater. Barefoot, though. And maybe it was her bare feet that reminded him of the rest of her that'd been bare.

Who was he kidding?

He didn't need to see her feet to think of that. Sex with Lyla seemed to be permanently on his mind now, and it didn't help that he'd had her only hours earlier.

Wyatt leaned in. Kissed her. And because he liked that little purring sound she made, he kissed her again.

"When you look at me," she asked, "do you think of your late wife?"

"No." He only saw Lyla here, and that created a new flurry of guilt inside him. He'd loved Ann for so long. For years. And he still loved her. However, he could feel a tug in his heart telling him it was time to let go.

But he couldn't.

Letting go hurt too much.

Lyla took his hand, put it on her belly. "What about the baby? Does that make you think of Ann?"

Not nearly enough. In fact, he was having a hard time wrapping his mind around anything but Lyla and this child. Still, Wyatt shook his head. Best not to share that with Lyla.

"The baby's like a gift from Ann," Lyla continued. "A gift for both of us. We'll both get the child we always wanted."

He knew where this was going—back to the subject of their wanting this child so much that they'd end up fighting for custody.

"We can stay married," Wyatt suggested, cutting her off at the pass while he continued to glance at the window and the security screen. "Raise this child together."

She stared at him. What she didn't do was jump to take him up on that offer.

"Earlier, before Billy called, you said you were about to tell me what you felt on the *inside,*" he reminded her. Maybe that would get her to consider his offer.

More staring. "I'm falling in love with you." And with that bolt from the blue delivered, she got up and moved away from him. She didn't look at him. Lyla kept her back to him. "I don't want to feel it. You don't want me to feel it, either. But I can't seem to stop it."

Well, hell. It had to stop.

Didn't it?

Part of him realized this would be a good thing for the baby. But sure as heck not for Lyla. Or even for him. Because he wasn't sure he could ever love her in return. That would make for a very uncomfortable arrangement.

"I'm offering to be your husband," he settled for saying. "And a full-time father for this child."

She looked over her shoulder at him. "It's not enough, Wyatt."

For such simple words, they packed a punch. A hard one. "Are you saying you'll leave?"

"I won't continue this sham of a marriage after the danger's over."

There it was. The threat he'd been trying to dodge since he learned the baby was indeed his. Because if she walked out, the baby went right along with her. Yeah, he could fight her and win. But the cost of winning would be pretty damn high.

A beep pierced through the room, and Wyatt pushed the conversation aside so he could hurry back to the window and the laptop. He didn't see anything unusual outside so he searched through the images on the screen, but he saw only the ranch hands.

And a blank spot.

Where there should have been some camera feed.

Wyatt's phone buzzed, and Busby's name popped up on the screen.

"What happened?" Wyatt immediately asked the ranch hand.

"Not sure, but I'm taking two of the men with me, and we're going out for a look at the west fence. That's where the sensor was tripped and the camera's out."

"Let me know if you spot anything."

There weren't any other precautions to take. The blinds were closed, and he'd already warned Lyla to stay away from the windows. Still, Wyatt turned off the lights and kept his gun ready.

Lyla's breathing had kicked up a significant notch by

the time she made it to him, and she watched the screen over his shoulder.

But there wasn't much to see.

There was no movement around Dallas's or Harlan's house. Still no one visible in any of the pastures, except for the ranch hands. There was one man standing guard on the back porch and another on the front. Both men were bundled in heavy coats and were carrying rifles to protect their home.

Home.

She probably thought of this place as the opposite of that. Nearly every minute she'd been here, Lyla had been in danger or in bed with him.

And she was still in danger.

She'd already said she would leave when it was safe to, but Wyatt knew she wouldn't just leave. She'd try to run, and even though he couldn't let her do that, he would have tried to do the same thing in her position.

It didn't take long for Busby and the two hands to disappear from view and into that blank space. Wyatt held his breath. Prayed. And he wished he could somehow divide himself and be out there to help them while protecting Lyla, too.

Even though Wyatt had been expecting the call, the buzzing sound from his phone still shot through him, and he immediately jabbed the button to answer it.

"False alarm," Busby said. "A tree limb fell on the camera and took it out. Looks like it's too damaged to fix."

Normally, that wouldn't have given Wyatt much cause for concern. After all, it was winter and downed tree limbs were common.

But this situation was far from normal.

"You're sure the limb wasn't tossed there?" Wyatt asked.

"Can't be sure of that at all, but I don't see anyone out here."

"Okay." That helped ease the tension a little. "Come on back to the house," Wyatt told Busby. "But keep watch." He didn't have to tell the man that this could turn into an ambush.

Or even something worse.

"I'll call Dallas, too," Busby offered, "and let him know what's going on. Keep watch on that computer screen."

"I will." In fact, Wyatt didn't intend to take his eyes off it.

Lyla sat on the edge of the desk, her attention nailed to the laptop, as well. Her breathing was way too fast, and Wyatt touched the back of her hand in an effort to soothe her.

"Are Kirby and Stella watching this?" she asked.

"Probably."

There was another laptop in Kirby's room where they were waiting and keeping watch. And if they were indeed seeing what was going on, Kirby would call Dallas for an update. Even though Kirby and Wyatt hadn't talked about it, his foster father knew that Lyla would be in the room with him. Listening to every word. Kirby would want to do whatever it took not to add more stress to what had already been too much for Lyla and the baby.

Wyatt was torn between staying put with Lyla so he could keep watching out the window or going to Stella and Kirby. Maybe if something did go wrong, he'd get enough of a heads up so he could hurry to them while still protecting Lyla.

The seconds crawled by with no sign of Busby and

the other men. Wyatt knew they probably weren't moving fast because they'd want to be able to hear if anything went wrong around them, but the wait was almost unbearable.

Finally, Wyatt saw the men come into range of a working camera. He had a clear view of them thanks to the lights they had fixed onto their hats. They weren't too far from the house now, and each step put them closer to being out of the line of a possible attack.

"Maybe it really was just a fallen limb," Lyla whispered, releasing the long breath she'd been holding.

Wyatt released a breath, too, but then he saw something that tightened every muscle in his body.

The shadows.

Not in front of the men. But behind them where their lights didn't reach.

There was just enough of a moon for Wyatt to make out the trees and underbrush on the camera feed.

"It could be the wind moving the tree branches," he said, hoping. Praying even more.

But then he saw something else. Another shadow, and it didn't mesh with the movement of the trees.

Without taking his eyes off the screen, Wyatt called Busby. "We might have a problem," he said the moment that Busby answered. "I think there might be somebody trailing along behind you."

"You're sure?"

"No—"

But Wyatt had to take back that answer. Because the shadows moved again. Thanks to the wind fanning the branches, he got a glimpse of something he sure as hell didn't want to see.

Two men dressed all in black.

And they were armed.

Chapter Sixteen

"Get out of there now!" Wyatt ordered Busby.

Lyla's throat snapped shut.

No. This couldn't be happening.

The killer was supposed to go after the fake evidence in the CSI van. He wasn't supposed to send his henchmen here to the ranch. But Lyla couldn't think of who else would be out skulking around on a bitter winter night. And there was no doubt about it—those men *were* skulking.

Wyatt had no sooner hung up with Busby when his phone buzzed again, and it was Dallas's name on the screen.

"I see them," Dallas said the moment Wyatt answered and put the call on speaker.

Busby and the two ranch hands pushed their horses in a gallop, racing back. The two men behind them, however, didn't run. They just continued to move through the pasture, using whatever they could for cover.

Making their way toward the house where Wyatt, Kirby, Stella and she were.

"I'll make sure Kirby and Stella stay down and take cover on the side of the fireplace in his room," Dallas offered. "And that all the ranch hands are inside. I can be there in five minutes."

"No," Wyatt said, surprising Lyla that he'd turn down backup. "This could be some kind of trap. They aren't shooting at anyone, so it could be a ploy to lure you away from the others."

"But Lyla and you seem to be the target," Dallas argued.

"And they could use any one of you to draw us out."

Mercy, she hadn't thought of that. There was no way Wyatt would sit still if his family came under attack.

"Besides, I don't want anyone out in the open right now," Wyatt added. "Just stay where you are and keep watch."

Wyatt was right. Dallas could be shot if he tried to get to them, and it would leave his own family more vulnerable. Heaven knew what they were all going through right now, because they had to be watching this possible threat unfold on the security screen.

"What do we do?" she asked Wyatt, and cursed the fear crawling through her.

He opened the desk drawer, took out a gun and handed it to her. "If they come closer to the house, you'll need to go in the bathroom and get in the shower."

It was lined with river rock similar to the fireplace that Stella and Kirby could use for cover. An attractive feature, but in this case, both could be good shields against bullets.

"You'll go in the shower with me," she said, and she tried not to make it sound like a question.

"I'll stay safe," he promised her, but there was no way he could guarantee he'd keep that promise.

Wyatt pulled her down for a kiss. Much too quick. But he had to keep his mind on the screen. Kisses, even those just to help keep her calm, were a big distraction.

Lyla said a prayer of thanks when Busby and the

ranch hands made it back to the house. Busby unlocked the front door, disarming the security system just long enough so they could get inside the foyer. The other hand went to the back and inside an enclosed porch.

So, everyone was safe and inside.

Well, inside anyway.

"There are three of them," Wyatt said.

It took her a moment to understand, and see, what he meant. The third man came into view of the camera. He was also dressed in black, his face was covered with something and he was armed.

Was this the killer? And had he sent his henchmen on ahead of him? If so, why?

The approaching gunmen were clearly outnumbered. Stella and Kirby were no doubt armed. Wyatt and she were. Ditto for the ranch hands. That meant it was seven-to-three odds. Knowing that should have eased some of the tension that was rifling through her body.

But it didn't.

Wyatt and she exchanged a glance, and she saw on his face the same concern she felt. Maybe there were more than three possible attackers, but there was no one else they could call for backup. At least no one that could make a fast response. The sheriff and one of his deputies were with Declan and Slade, and that probably left only one other deputy to protect the town. And he was with Billy.

The phone buzzed again, and even though Lyla had been expecting a call from one of his brothers, the sound still caused her to gasp. However, when she looked at the screen, her stomach dropped.

Unknown caller.

Someone had blocked the number and name, and she doubted they'd done that for any good reason. It wasn't one of the three men in the pasture, either, because Lyla could see them on the security camera, and none was on the phone.

"Marshal McCabe," Wyatt answered.

It seemed to take an eternity for someone to speak on the other end of the line, but finally she heard the voice. "It's me," the man said.

Lyla shook her head and looked at Wyatt to see if it was someone he recognized. It wasn't.

"Who the hell is this?" Wyatt demanded.

"Nicky Garnett."

The gunman who'd shot at them at her house. A very dangerous man and someone almost certainly connected to the men in the pasture.

Men who were now running.

What was happening? Was this the start of the attack that they'd been dreading?

"What do you want?" Wyatt asked Nicky.

"To give you a little warning." There was no urgency in the man's voice. In fact, he seemed pleased about the threat Lyla was sure was coming. "If I were you, I'd get my bride and anyone else out of the house."

"And why would I do that?"

"Remember that maid you put on paid leave?" Nicky didn't wait for Wyatt to respond. "Well, she had some family problems that required her to come up with a big chunk of cash. Cash that my boss gladly provided her for services rendered."

Lyla pressed her fingers to her mouth to stop the gasp, and everything inside her went completely still.

Wyatt's grip tightened on the phone until his knuckles were white. "What the hell did she do?"

"For one thing, she put a tiny camera with infrared technology on one of the outside windowsills. It made it pretty easy for us to know that you and Lyla aren't in that heavily guarded van heading to San Antonio."

Sweet heaven. That meant Nicky and his boss would know exactly who was in the house. And the infrared would pick up on their specific location. It would make it easier for them to target them with long-range rifles.

Like the ones the men who were nearing the house had.

Wyatt and his family had been so careful making sure the place was secure, but it would have been easy to miss a small camera. Now they might pay a high price for that.

"One more thing," Nicky said, his voice still calm but yet cold as ice. "We had the maid set a bomb, too. A bomb with a timer like the one we used at Rocky Creek."

Lyla could have sworn her heart stopped for several seconds, and then it slammed against her ribs.

"Where is it?" Wyatt demanded through clenched teeth. "Where's the bomb?"

"Very near to you. And if my calculations are right, you've got less than five minutes before you're all blown to smithereens."

"Where is it? Where'd she put the bomb?" Wyatt shouted into the phone. But he was talking to himself because Nicky Garnett had already hung up.

Hell, no. This couldn't be happening.

"What do we do?" Lyla asked, the terror spiking her voice.

Wyatt tried not to panic. Tried to think. This could all be a trap to get them out of the house, but he'd seen the destruction the bomb had done at Rocky Creek. If one that size detonated here, the house could be destroyed and everyone inside killed.

"Come on." Wyatt drew his gun and got them running

out of the room and down the stairs. He slapped off lights along the way so they couldn't be pinpointed by a shooter using a long-range rifle. Of course, if Nicky had told the truth, they were being tracked with infrared, which allowed them to be tracked no matter where they went.

"We have to get out," Wyatt told Busby and the other ranch hand in the foyer. "The place might blow up."

Wyatt had a split-second debate with himself about having them come with Lyla and him, but the nearest vehicle was his truck, and there wouldn't be room in the cab.

"Go to the mare's barn," Wyatt told the men. That was at the front of the property by the road, and they'd be able to see if anyone drove up. "But watch out for those guys moving in the pasture. They're armed."

That was the only warning he had time to issue. While they hurried to Kirby's room, he phoned Dallas to fill him in. "Nicky Garnett just called. There could be a bomb."

Dallas cursed. "He's probably lying through his teeth."

"Yeah, but I can't take that chance. It's me, don't shoot!" Wyatt called out. He threw open the door to Kirby's room and spotted Stella and him, both armed, huddled by the fireplace. He motioned for them to get to their feet. "Nicky said they have infrared, and if they do, they know exactly what we're doing now. But I can't see them. The laptop will lose the internet connection once I'm out of the house."

"I'm on my way," Dallas said, repeating his earlier offer.

Like before, though, Wyatt had to turn him down. "Too risky. If they'd wanted us dead, they would have just blown us up. They wouldn't have given us a warning or time to get out."

So, what did they want?

Wyatt figured it had something to do with that fake tape. He'd been so sure the killer would follow that trail.

But he'd been dead wrong.

And in doing so, he'd put Lyla and the baby in grave danger again.

"Stay where you are and keep monitoring the security systems," Wyatt told Dallas. They hurried through the house and toward the back. "I'm taking Stella, Kirby and Lyla to the truck. I left it parked right out by the back steps. And we'll come to you. That way, I can drop them off and face down whoever's out there."

"No!" Lyla insisted. "You can't sacrifice yourself for us."

Yes, he could. For them and the baby, he would do whatever it took. But it wasn't a sacrifice he had in mind. "I'm a good shot," he reminded her. "And unlike those men, I know every inch of this ranch. I can stop this."

"And you could be taking the danger to Dallas and the others. I'm the one who's drawing the trouble here. I'm the one they want."

Probably. But Wyatt didn't have time to argue with her. "The bomb could hurt the baby," he said. "Or worse."

Yeah, it was brutal, and even in the darkness he could see the color drain from her face. But it worked. It got her moving, which in turn got Stella and Kirby moving. Kirby was still a little shaky on his feet, but Stella looped her arm around his waist and helped him walk. Wyatt grabbed the keys from the peg near the door and hurried with them onto the back porch.

"Run," Wyatt told the ranch hand. "Go to the hay barn and keep watch from there."

The guy frantically bobbed his head and practically sprinted away.

Wyatt moved fast, too, and crammed the others into the truck. They were nearly on top of each other, but it wouldn't be a long drive to Dallas's place.

"Maybe they set more than one bomb," Stella said, looking up at the house and then the grounds.

"They don't want us dead," Wyatt repeated, and he prayed that was true.

He threw the truck into gear and gunned the engine. Just as his phone buzzed.

"Answer it," he told Lyla. And she somehow managed to get it from his pocket.

"It's me, Busby," Wyatt heard him say the moment Lyla put the call on speaker. "We got a problem, boss. I just had a look through the binoculars. The ones with night vision. And I can see at least three men on the road that leads to Dallas's house."

Wyatt's heart went to his knees. "Where exactly?"

"They're not on the ranch grounds, which explains why they didn't trip the sensors. They're just on the other side of the fence. And they appear to be carrying long-range rifles."

That was not what Wyatt wanted to hear. Especially since that was the direction they were headed. Wyatt slammed on the brakes.

"Change of plans," Wyatt said to Busby. He was aware that Stella and Lyla were terrified, but he couldn't take the time to assure them now. "I'm heading to the barn behind the house. Call Dallas and tell him what's going on."

Wyatt didn't wait for Busby to agree. Without pushing the end-call button on the phone, he hit the accelerator and got them heading toward the barn. He had to put some distance between the house and them in case of an explosion. They were still close enough to be hurt.

"Hold on," Wyatt told them. "And get as far down on the seat as you can."

The barn doors were closed. There were no animals inside because it was used for storage during winter months. And so that he wouldn't have to get out, Wyatt planned to drive through the wooden doors.

Lyla, Stella and Kirby were still scrambling to get down when the truck slammed into the doors and sent them flying off their hinges. The air bags deployed, slapping into them. But even over that noise and the roar of the engine, Wyatt heard something he damn sure didn't want to hear.

Someone fired a shot.

Chapter Seventeen

The fear jolted through Lyla.

Because she knew what that sound meant.

They were under fire again.

She looked up just as a bullet came through the back window of the truck. It went straight through, shattering the windshield. The glass cracked and webbed and made it impossible to see.

However, she had no trouble hearing.

Not just the second shot, either, but also Wyatt's profanity when he shoved her back lower onto the seat. There wasn't much room, with the four of them and the air bags, but he squeezed them as low as he could manage.

What she didn't hear was an explosion, and they were still plenty close enough to the house that if there'd been one, she would have known about it. Of course, they didn't know yet if Nicky had lied to them, to get them out of the house. But it could have just as easily been a real bomb, so Lyla didn't regret their decision to leave.

Well, not yet anyway.

They had to make it out of this alive first.

"Find out where the shooters are!" Wyatt shouted, and it took her a moment to realize he was talking to Busby and not one of them.

She couldn't hear what the ranch hand said, but Lyla figured the shooters weren't the ones Busby had spotted near the road leading to Dallas's house. No. These shots had almost certainly come from the trio they'd seen earlier on the security cameras. They could have easily made it to the area by the barn by now.

The shots kept coming, and Wyatt crawled over her to shield her with his body. She hated that he was taking the risks. Hated even more that there was nothing she could do about it. They had to protect the baby and that meant protecting her.

One of the bullets slammed through the back of the truck and into the dashboard. The air bags stopped any debris from flying at them, but whoever was shooting was literally tearing the truck apart.

"We have to move," Wyatt said, taking the words right out of her mouth. They'd die if they stayed put.

The truck was in the open doorway, and they needed to get to the side of the barn. Unfortunately, if the shooters were using infrared, they would still be able to target them, but maybe they could use something as a shield until someone could stop the gunmen.

With the engine still running, Wyatt turned the steering wheel to the left, maneuvering them out of the doorway. It took some effort, and it didn't help when the bullets continued to come at them nonstop. Clearly, these men had come prepared to kill them.

Maybe.

Like the other attack, most of the shots were going into the top and sides of the vehicle. Only the one to the dash had come close, and it was possible that it'd been misfired.

Did that mean this was another kidnapping attempt? If so, then she was no doubt the target.

Not exactly a comforting thought, especially since these goons were likely prepared to kill everyone else to get to her. And why? At this point if she got anywhere near the real evidence, it could be discredited.

Maybe that was the point.

She could taint it by association.

The second that Wyatt had the truck maneuvered out of the entrance, he threw open his door. "Come on."

And that was the only warning Lyla got before he took hold of her arm and pulled her from the truck. They landed in an open stall that was strewed with hay. Kirby and Stella piled in right behind them.

The cold was instant and sent her teeth chattering, a reminder that she hadn't grabbed her coat when they'd run. Of course, staying warm hadn't exactly been a high priority with the bomb threat.

"We should get into the tack room," Kirby insisted. Like her, he was shivering. Stella, too. And with everything Kirby had been through recently, that couldn't be good. This might cause him to have some kind of relapse in his recovery.

The shots didn't stop. They continued to pelt the truck, but thankfully none of them were coming in their direction. Not yet anyway. But it seemed to her that the shooters were moving, probably coming closer to them.

Wyatt tipped his head to a walled over area in the center of the barn. "The tack room," he told her.

Not the standard place to keep tack, but the barn was far bigger than most and clearly used for storage now since inside there were some all-terrain vehicles, a boat and even a travel trailer. None of it would give them much protection, but what it did do was give them plenty of places to hide. And with only one way in, that meant the shooters would have to come to them.

"Let's go," Wyatt ordered.

They stayed close to the side of the barn, out of the path of the gaping hole in the door, and once they made it to the room filled with saddles and other riding gear, Wyatt got them inside.

Not himself, though.

He leaned out, looking for those shooters.

"I still don't see them," he said to Busby, and waited while the man spoke. "Well, find them."

Wyatt hit the end-call button and rammed his phone back in his pocket. "The gunmen took out the security cameras. We have no way to monitor them."

Sweet heaven. That meant they could be anywhere, but she was betting they were sneaking up on the barn. Those shots were definitely getting closer.

"Stay back," Wyatt warned her when she tried to pull him deeper inside with the rest of them.

And without warning, the shots stopped.

Because she had her hand on Wyatt's left arm, she felt his muscles freeze, and his breath seemed to stop for a second. Only then did he ease back, and he put his finger to his mouth in a *stay quiet* gesture.

Lyla heard another sound.

Footsteps.

The gunmen had arrived.

She tried to level her breathing. Tried not to move. So she wouldn't do anything to give away their position. Beside her, Stella and Kirby did the same, but if any of them made a sound, the gunmen would hear them.

The room was much larger than the truck, but Wyatt was blocking the doorway. Again, protecting them. However, it prevented any of them from moving beside him and taking aim. Something he almost certainly didn't want them to do anyway, but Lyla hated that all she could do was sit there and wait for this nightmare to play out.

Judging from the sound of the footsteps, the men kept coming closer. Wyatt held steady. Definitely not shaking like she was, and he leaned out just a fraction.

And fired.

The sound blasted through the barn. Through her, too. There was a groan of pain followed by the sound of someone thudding to the ground.

Wyatt had obviously managed to take out one of the men. Lyla was both relieved and thankful.

But not for long.

"Marshal?" someone shouted. And this time she recognized the voice. It was Nicky again. "I think it's time we had a little talk."

Wyatt didn't answer, but the smugness in Nicky's voice had her heart racing. He didn't seem like a man who had any doubts about this plan he'd just put into place.

"Who hired you to come here?" Kirby shouted. "Was it Travis Weston?"

"No. I don't work for him. Got me a new boss now, who pays a lot better."

Maybe a lie, but it could be the truth. From everything she'd heard Wyatt say about him, Nicky wasn't the sort to stay loyal. He was a follow-the-money kind of hired killer.

"Why don't you tell them you're here?" Nicky said.

Wyatt glanced at her to see if she knew what he meant, but Lyla had to shake her head.

"Go ahead," Nicky said. "Why don't you show the marshal what you got there?"

"I'm sorry, Wyatt," she heard another man say.

Billy.

Good grief, what was he doing here?

Like her, he sounded terrified. Of course, he could be faking it if he was the mastermind behind this plan.

"I'm sorry," Billy repeated. "But this is something you have to see."

Despite the hold she had on his arm, Wyatt leaned out just slightly.

And he cursed.

Lyla desperately wanted to see what had caused Wyatt to react that way, but she stayed put. And quiet.

"It's a detonator," Billy said, his voice barely audible over the sudden howling of the wind.

Oh, God. A timer for what? Was there actually a bomb after all?

"I got it mixed up a little when I told you the maid had set a bomb," Nicky mocked. "She did. But not at the ranch. It's beneath Dallas's house, where most of your family is holed up. Get out here now, or the bomb goes off, and everyone inside that house dies."

WYATT HAD FELT FEAR before, but this was a whole new level. He thought of his brothers Dallas, Clayton and Harlan. All in the house. Their wives, too, along with Slade's wife and Declan's fiancée. And the children.

All babies.

And now they were in danger.

Well, they were if Nicky was telling the truth.

"Billy?" Wyatt called out. "Is there really a detonator?"

"Afraid so. I didn't mean for this to happen. They grabbed me when I got to the sheriff's office and then forced me to call the deputy to tell him that I'd changed my mind about staying there."

So, this plan had been in motion for several hours. Before the CSI van had even arrived.

"Step out!" Nicky insisted. "Or I push this little button and a whole lot of marshals die tonight."

It was a huge risk, but Wyatt had no choice. "Stay put," he warned Lyla and the others.

"No!" she practically shouted. She tried to stop him, but Wyatt stepped out anyway.

Yeah, it was a detonator, all right.

And it was clipped to Nicky's belt like a badge.

If Billy was in on this little plan, then he was giving a fine acting job, because thanks to the headlights on the truck, Wyatt could see that the man was pale and shaking. He was also cuffed, with his hands in front of his body.

Nicky looked as calm and cocky as he'd sounded on the phone. He was also armed and had his gun pointed at Wyatt. He had his other hand on the detonator. In fact, his index finger was poised right over the button.

Wyatt glanced at the hole where the door had once been, and he spotted one of the gunmen. His rifle was pointed right at Billy. The other gunman was dead on the ground.

"Don't give me a reason to press this button," Nicky warned.

"Who's behind this?" Wyatt asked before Nicky could say anything else.

"Maybe I am."

"Not enough brains. And no motive. The person behind this wants to hide their involvement in Webb's murder."

A flash of anger went through Nicky's eyes. That *not enough brains* insult had pushed his buttons, and even though Wyatt didn't personally know the man, he appeared to have a short fuse. Not good, since he controlled the detonator.

"Well, I hope you're getting paid enough," Wyatt added, "because attempted murder is going to send you away for a long, long time."

"Only if I'm caught, which I don't intend to happen. Now shut up and listen to how this is going to work. You and Lyla will come with me, and Kirby will get the detonator. Your brothers and their families will be safe."

"But not my wife," Wyatt argued.

"She'll be safe as long as she cooperates. And all she has to do is alter the voice on the tape that's being delivered to the lab as we speak."

Wyatt didn't believe Nicky for a minute about Lyla being safe after she cooperated. She would be a loose end, and while they might not kill her instantly, eventually the killer would want her eliminated.

"Why didn't you just go after the CSI van?" Wyatt asked.

"Too risky. Lyla's a better bet, and she'll probably be happy to cooperate rather than risk endangering that baby's she's carrying."

Wyatt didn't have to see Lyla's face to know that it sent a shock of fear through her. It went through him, too. And not just fear. Pure, raw anger. How dare this SOB threaten his unborn child?

"How'd you know about the baby?" Wyatt snapped. "Are you the one who stole the embryo?"

Nicky chuckled. "Wish I could take credit for that, but, no, my boss hired someone else to do it."

Another lackey. What Wyatt needed was the identity of the person responsible for all this chaos.

"Let's get in your truck," Nicky instructed. "Me, you and Lyla. And one of my helpers, who's waiting outside, will climb in the back with Billy. The other helper will stay here with Kirby, Stella and the detonator."

"Why take Billy?" Wyatt asked.

"Because I know too much," Billy answered. "Or so he thinks. He believes that I listened to the tape recording of the murder. I didn't."

"Yeah. Because he says it's fake," Nicky grumbled. "Like we're gonna believe that."

Well, he should. It was the truth, but Wyatt seriously doubted he could convince Nicky or his boss of that now. And it meant Billy was soon to be a dead man, too—unless he was the person behind this. But that didn't make sense, because Billy knew the tape wasn't real.

Wyatt had to figure a way out of this. But how? If he dove at Nicky, the guy with the rifle would just shoot him, and that would leave Lyla and the others without anyone to protect them. It was entirely possible that Dallas and Slade were on their way to help him, but Wyatt prayed they'd somehow gotten news of the possible bomb and were evacuating.

"Get moving now!" Nicky ordered.

Billy's gaze met Wyatt's, and even though he wasn't sure what Billy intended to do, the one thing that couldn't happen was for the killer to get his hands on Lyla.

Wyatt gave Billy a slight nod, and he braced himself for whatever was about to happen.

And it happened fast.

Despite the cuffs, Billy grabbed on to Nicky's hand, snapping it away from the detonator. Wyatt didn't waste a second. He pivoted and aimed at the man with the rifle and fired before he could.

The man went down.

Wyatt hoped he was dead or at least incapable of

firing that rifle, because he didn't have time to disarm him. He launched himself into the fray with Billy and Nicky, but he had to drop his own gun to use both hands to try to restrain Nicky and to keep his finger off the detonator.

He sensed the movement behind him and cursed. Lyla was out of the tack room, trying to take aim at Nicky. But Wyatt didn't want her out in the open.

With a firm grip on Nicky's left hand, Wyatt managed to punch him. Hard. It was enough for Nicky's head to flop back, and Wyatt reached for the man's gun.

But the sound stopped him cold.

"Hold it right there, Wyatt," someone said. "Move another inch, and you're a dead man."

Chapter Eighteen

Even though she was only inches away from grabbing Nicky's gun from the barn floor, Lyla froze. Because the man who'd spoken that warning meant business.

It was Sheriff Zeke Mercer.

And he had a semiautomatic pointed right at Wyatt.

With just a glance of his narrowed gaze, Zeke issued a firm threat. If she tried to help, Wyatt would pay the price. And Zeke would shoot him, because in his mind, Wyatt was likely expendable.

All of them were.

Well, she would be after she faked that evidence. After that, she and her baby would be expendable, too.

"Get up," Zeke ordered Wyatt. "And move away from Nicky. Our ride should be here any minute now, and we'll be leaving."

Wyatt did get up, slow and easy, and he volleyed glances between Zeke and the detonator. Nicky got up, too, retrieved his gun and pointed it not at Wyatt but at her. He knew that was the only way to keep Wyatt from going after him again.

And it worked.

She saw the fear, and the frustration, tighten Wyatt's entire body.

"Told you I had a new boss," Nicky bragged. "No

way would I go back to work for Travis. Not with what Zeke pays me. And besides, me working for Zeke puts the blame right back on Travis. That's why Zeke even pretended to rat out my location when he called you. But before he made that call, he had me in some place where the law would never get to me."

"Shut up," Zeke told the man, and he looked at Wyatt. "Now call Dallas and tell him to stay put," Zeke instructed. "Not just him, all of them. Because we'll detonate the bomb if any of them show up here. Oh, and put the call on speaker and don't mention my name or the bomb. Because I will kill you if you do. And then I'll kill all of them."

That wasn't a bluff. Neither was the bomb. That was probably why Wyatt made the call. "Stay away from the barn," Wyatt told his brother. "I want the ranch hands kept back, too."

"What's going on?" Dallas demanded.

"Something that I have to ask you and the others to stay out of." And with that, Wyatt put his phone in his shirt pocket, his gaze fixed on Zeke. "There's no need for this."

Zeke shook his head, and despite the cold wind battering him, he stayed put in the shattered doorway. "Yeah, there is a need."

"Because it'll be your voice on that tape," Lyla continued when he didn't add more. "Except there isn't a tape."

"Oh, there is. Sarah made one. She used to threaten me with it whenever she thought I might tell anyone what'd happened that night. It's the reason Billy's coming with us. I'll let Nicky get the truth out of him, because I'm betting Sarah put copies somewhere. And I have to find those copies and destroy them."

If Sarah had indeed done that, the copies hadn't turned

up, and Billy genuinely didn't seem to know where they'd be. Of course, that didn't matter. He'd die because of this after they tortured him to get information that he didn't even have.

"Sarah could have been bluffing," Lyla pointed out. "In fact, it could have been her insurance policy to keep you from coming after her."

That realization flashed through Zeke's eyes. Not a good realization, either, because he had to be thinking this was all for nothing.

"You killed my mother," Billy said. His voice wasn't too steady. Neither was he, and he looked ready to launch himself at Zeke.

"No, I did," Nicky volunteered. "Sneaked into the hospital and then had my girlfriend call those other idiots and set them up. It was Zeke's idea to go to the hospital, too, so he wouldn't look guilty."

"But you are guilty," Wyatt stated through clenched teeth. "Let me guess. You and Webb had a falling-out over a business deal, and you were more than happy to help Sarah kill him."

Zeke didn't say a word. He only glanced behind him, no doubt looking for the vehicle that would come and collect them. Once they were away from the ranch, it was likely that the bomb would be detonated anyway.

Too many potential witnesses to leave behind.

"Webb got greedy. He wanted more of the cut they were making from the gunrunning that they were doing with some of the boys from Rocky Creek," Nicky said, ignoring the glare that Zeke shot him.

Zeke suddenly didn't seem nearly as confident and cocky as his hired gun, and he kept glancing back, looking for the vehicle.

Maybe one of the ranch hands or Wyatt's brothers

had managed to stop it. She hoped so, because once the vehicle arrived, their chances of escaping dwindled considerably.

"And what about Travis and Greg?" Wyatt asked. "Did they have anything to do with this?"

"No, but I wish Travis had," Zeke mumbled. "I would have loved seeing his arrogant butt behind bars."

"That's the pot calling the kettle black. You killed my father for money," Billy spat out. "You had no right to kill him. No one did."

Zeke huffed. "You remember how he used to beat on you? And on you?" he added, tipping his head to Wyatt.

"I remember," Wyatt answered, "but that isn't why you killed him. It's because he wanted a bigger cut of the illegal money you two were making."

"I'm not admitting to anything," Zeke snarled.

No, but the admission was there and unspoken. There would have been no reason for him to kill Sarah unless it was to cover up the fact that he was an accessory to murder.

"Did you ever see the recording that Sarah made?" Lyla pressed, though it was too late to convince Zeke that the recording didn't exist. Still, she might be able to distract him in some way.

"No. But she said she had it hidden away where I could never find it. She said she recorded the tape during one of our conversations and that I'd mentioned something about my business dealings with her husband."

"But not his murder," Lyla pressed.

His forehead bunched up, and Zeke stopped, looking even more uneasy about all that he'd set into motion. He glanced up the road again. "The van's here. Time to leave." And he motioned for Lyla to come closer.

Wyatt stepped in front of her. "Webb deserved to die, but we don't. Not just to cover up your crime."

"You're wrong. I'm not going to jail for anything. I'll cover my tracks any way I need to."

"That included having your goon kill my mother." Billy's hands tightened into fists.

Zeke didn't seem to notice Billy's reaction. The lights of the vehicle slashed through the hole and into the barn, and Zeke had to turn his eyes away. It was just a split-second distraction.

And the only one necessary.

With a feral sound screaming from his throat, Billy dove toward Zeke, crashing into the man and knocking him to the ground.

Nicky reacted, fast, moving toward his boss to protect him. But Wyatt reacted, too. He lunged forward, trying to catch onto Nicky's arm before he could press the detonator.

Lyla started to move, too, but she didn't get far before the sound stopped her.

A shot blasted through the barn.

WYATT PRAYED THAT the bullet hadn't gone anywhere near Lyla, but he couldn't look back to see if it had. Suddenly, he was in another fight with Nicky, and the man was still trying to hit that damn button on the detonator.

Nicky outweighed him by a good forty pounds, but he didn't have nearly the motivation that Wyatt had. Lyla, the baby and his family were in danger, and he had to stop this dirt wad from killing them all. Of course, that wouldn't stop the danger if he couldn't do something about Zeke.

But one fight at a time.

Wyatt took hold of Nicky's left hand, but the man kept

a death grip on his gun. Wyatt's own weapon was just out of reach, and he could let go of Nicky to get it. Lyla must have realized that because she rushed forward to help.

"Stay back," Wyatt yelled.

She didn't listen. Of course. Later, he'd chew her out for that. But she kicked the gun closer to his hand just as Nicky punched him so hard that Wyatt swore he saw stars. Before Wyatt could snatch up his gun, he heard the blast.

It was too close.

Maybe right at Lyla.

God. His heart skipped some beats, and he looked back, expecting to see the worst. But instead he saw Kirby. He was standing in the tack room door, his gun aimed at Nicky. He'd been the one to fire the shot and looked ready to fire a second.

But it wasn't necessary.

Nicky was dead.

"Get the detonator," Wyatt told Lyla. "Then stay down on the ground. There'll be gunmen in that van." He grabbed his Colt and raced toward Billy and Zeke, who were still in a scuffle on the floor.

"You need to tell Dallas to evacuate," she called out to him.

"Dallas knows. I left my phone on after Zeke had me make that call. Dallas would have heard everything."

He hoped. That was the plan anyway when Wyatt had risked not pressing the end-call button. If Zeke had noticed, he probably would have killed him.

And that's exactly what he was trying to do to Billy now—kill him. Zeke had managed to hang on to his weapon and was trying to aim it so he could shoot Billy.

Outside the barn, Wyatt heard familiar voices. Busby, Dallas and Slade. He maneuvered himself around Billy and Zeke so he could stop the gunmen in the van from coming inside after them. But he looked out in just enough time to see Dallas slam one of the men against the van.

"Is everyone out of your house?" Wyatt asked him.

"Yeah. Thanks for the heads-up."

Later Wyatt would say *you're welcome*. But for now, all hell was breaking loose, and Wyatt had to make sure that no one fired any shots near Lyla. He tried to take aim at Zeke, but his and Billy's bodies were in such a tangle that Wyatt didn't have a clean shot.

So, he waited, watched. With his heart pounding in his throat and with every inch of his body on alert. Finally, he saw an opening in the scuffle, and when he got the chance, Wyatt leaned in and bashed the butt of his gun against Zeke's head.

It worked.

The man stopped struggling, his hand dropping limply on the ground.

But Billy didn't stop. He latched on to Zeke's gun and came up, ready to fire. He took aim at Zeke's heart.

"This is for killing my mother," Billy said, putting his finger on the trigger.

"Don't," Wyatt warned him. Though he wasn't sure what to say to stop Billy. Zeke had killed both of his parents and was planning to kill him. Still, at the moment, Zeke was unarmed.

"You're not a murderer," Wyatt told Billy.

"But I want him dead. You should want him dead, too. He nearly killed Lyla and your baby."

"I know." And Wyatt had to tamp down the anger. No, it was rage. But the rage faded considerably when he felt Lyla's hand brush over his arm.

"Zeke will get his punishment in prison, Billy," Lyla

said. Her voice was soft. Almost soothing. He wasn't sure how he managed it, because when he looked into her eyes, Wyatt saw the aftermath of the fear that was no doubt mirrored in his.

"If you think this ends anything," Zeke snapped, "it doesn't." With venom in his eyes, he looked at Kirby, then Wyatt. "When I give my statement, I'll just tell everyone that you helped Sarah and me hide Webb's body."

"Then you'd be lying," Kirby said.

"Would I?" The corner of Zeke's mouth lifted into a twisted smile. "Something like that can follow a man around for a lifetime. Wouldn't hurt Kirby much, since he's retired, but all his boys would have to listen to the whispers about taking the law into their own hands. But if you convince Billy here to pull the trigger, then I'll have no statement to make."

Wyatt wanted his name cleared. His family's too. But not at the cost of coaxing Billy to kill an unarmed man.

"Not all lawmen are capable of murder," Kirby told Zeke.

Zeke chuckled. "Yeah. You are. So, what will it be? If I'm dead, there'll be no one to point a finger at you and these boys you've worked so hard to protect. And as for me, death would be welcome."

Yeah, because Zeke wouldn't end up in prison with men he'd help to put there. Even if they couldn't pin accessory to Webb's murder on Zeke, he would still be charged with orchestrating Sarah's murder and the attacks on Lyla and him. That would be a life sentence, at least, and with no possibility of parole.

The next moments crawled by. Billy, with the gun still ready to end Zeke's life. Zeke, staring up at them and not offering one bit of remorse or regret for anyone but himself.

But it didn't matter.

The realization hit Wyatt. It didn't matter why Zeke had done what he'd done. It only mattered that Lyla and his family were safe.

Wyatt extended his hand. "Billy, I need the gun." And he made sure he sounded like the lawman that he was. The one that Kirby had trained him to be.

With all eyes on him and with his hand shaking, Billy finally gave Wyatt the gun.

Wyatt released the breath he'd been holding, and while Kirby held Zeke at gunpoint, Wyatt pulled Lyla into his arms. The embrace didn't last long, and he barely had enough time to check and make sure she was okay.

There wasn't a scratch on her.

That was another prayer answered. There'd been a bunch of those tonight.

"These are the guys who were on the road near my place," Dallas explained, and Wyatt went out to help him contain the men who'd been in the van. "Sheriff Geary's on his way back to help us arrest every one of them. Zeke, too." He said the man's name as if it was profanity. "I want him taken to the marshals' office and thrown into jail."

Wyatt looked around. "We need to get a bomb squad out here to sweep every inch of the ranch." Which would mean they would all end up in town at a hotel for the night.

"You should see to Lyla." Dallas tipped his head toward her. "She doesn't look too steady on her feet."

She didn't. And even though there was plenty that Wyatt needed to be doing to get these gunmen off the property, he went to her.

Yeah, definitely not steady.

He hooked his arm around her and moved her against one of the barn posts. "What's wrong?"

She shook her head. "I just realized it's over."

Wyatt got the feeling she was talking about more than just the danger.

Lyla pulled away from him, dodged his gaze. "I can go home now."

Wyatt hadn't expected that to come out of her mouth. Not this soon. Only minutes earlier they'd survived a life-and-death situation, so he'd figured there'd be a little downtime to come to terms with everything that had happened.

Apparently not.

He was trying to figure out what to say, when his blasted phone buzzed again. Wyatt considered ignoring it, but then he saw his boss's name on the screen.

"We're making the arrests now," Wyatt answered, hoping to put a quick end to this.

"Good. But that's not why I'm calling," Saul answered back. "You should get down here to the marshals' office as soon as you can. There's something you and the others need to see."

Chapter Nineteen

Wyatt was a hundred percent sure he didn't want to deal with anything else tonight. Well, nothing that didn't involve talking to Lyla to figure out how he could fix this.

First, though, he needed to figure out what *this* was, exactly.

And it would have to wait until he found out what had arrived at the marshals' office. With the rotten luck he and his family had had lately, Wyatt prayed this wasn't another dose of bad news. They'd had enough of that to last a couple of lifetimes.

Wyatt pulled into the parking lot of the marshals' building. Not alone, either. Lyla and Stella were with him in his truck, and Kirby, his brothers and their families were in assorted vehicles that pulled in right behind them. Billy, too, had come along with them.

Saul probably hadn't intended the entire family to come to the office, but since they were all going to check in to the hotel just up the street, it wasn't exactly out of the way. Besides, none of his brothers probably wanted to be away from their wives and children.

Danger had a way making a person realize just what was important.

And in Lyla's case, apparently it had clarified for her

that she wanted to go home. Away from him. Away from the chaos that'd been her life for the past couple of days.

They huddled together against the cold and made their way into the building and up the stairs. Soon, there'd be reports to write up on the shooting, the deaths of the gunmen and Nicky Garnett. Reports of what Zeke had and hadn't confessed to. But Wyatt hoped that wasn't the reason Saul had called them all in.

After one glimpse of his boss's face, and hands, Wyatt knew that it was more than that. Saul was wearing gloves, the kind a marshal used when handling evidence.

Saul wasn't in his office but rather at Dallas's desk, which was toward the center of the sprawling squad room. "This arrived by courier about an hour ago."

There was a shipping box, and Saul reached inside and took out an old-fashioned cassette tape player.

"Sarah," Lyla mumbled.

Saul nodded. "Apparently, long before she went into a coma, she'd put this in a safe-deposit box in San Antonio and left instructions that it was to be delivered here in the event of her untimely death."

Well, it'd been untimely, all right.

"Nicky Garnett confessed to killing her, and he was working for Zeke," Billy said, walking closer. "So, there really was a tape?"

"Yeah. And I figured we'd all listen to it together."

Hell. They weren't out of the woods yet. Because if that was Sarah or Zeke on the recording, either one of them could implicate Kirby. Or one of the rest of them. It wouldn't even have to be true, but as Zeke had said—it could put a shadow over them for the rest of their lives.

Wyatt felt Lyla's arm go around his waist, and just that simple gesture felt far better than it should have. His brothers' wives did the same, despite the fact that Clayton's wife, Lenora, was holding their son. Slade and his wife, Maya, each held their babies.

"I want you to marry me," someone said out of the blue.

Kirby.

And he was looking directly at Stella.

Judging from the mumbles and sounds of surprise, no one in the room had been expecting that. And Wyatt hadn't expected Stella's reaction.

"You're proposing now?" Her hands went on her hips. "Why, because you think some lies on that tape will send one or all of us to jail?"

"I don't care what's on that tape," Kirby insisted. "It won't change how I feel about you. About any of you." He motioned around the room and then pried Stella's left hand off her hip so he could hold it in his. "I love you, and asking you to marry me is something I should have done a long time ago."

Stella's mouth opened as if she might question that. But how could she? Every one of them knew what Kirby had said was true. He'd been in love with her for years.

"You'd better say yes," Declan volunteered. "I'd like to attend my parents' wedding, and I'm sure your other sons and daughters-in-law feel the same."

No more sounds of surprise. Just nods and mumbles of approval.

There were tears in Stella's eyes now, and she went into Kirby's waiting arms. "Yes, I'll marry you."

Wyatt smiled in spite of Kirby's rotten timing. Except, Kirby had managed to inject some genuine happiness in what had been a hell of a bad day.

The hugs and well-wishes came. Lots of them. Everyone went over to hug their parents. It didn't matter that Declan was their only biological son—Kirby and Stella had been Mom and Dad to all of them. The only person who stayed back was Billy, his attention focused on the tape recorder on the desk.

"Should we listen to this tape now?" Saul prompted.

It was time.

But it wasn't.

Wyatt glanced around the room at his family's faces and knew there was something missing. Lyla. Who'd already told him she intended to go home.

"I want this to be your home," Wyatt blurted out to her. He said it a little louder than he'd intended. Actually, a lot louder, because suddenly everyone was looking at them.

"Not the marshals' office," he clarified, feeling very tongue-tied. "I want the ranch to be your home." He motioned around the room as Kirby had done. "And I want this to be your family."

Like Stella, she didn't jump to say yes. In fact, Lyla just stared at him. Then shook her head.

Damn. She was going to say no, and Wyatt didn't want that. So he stopped her with a kiss. In hindsight, it probably shouldn't have been so long and deep, but it hushed her, all right.

And left them both a little out of breath.

"I want you to marry me," Wyatt insisted.

"Uh, you're already married," Declan pointed out.

Yes, but in name only. Well, except for the one time they'd made love. But Wyatt wanted more. More than in name only. More than what he had with Lyla now.

"The baby is Ann and Wyatt's," Lyla said. Apparently, Wyatt wasn't the only one in a blurting mood.

"They know." Declan, again. "I told them."

"And we're all happy for Wyatt and you," Kirby said, coming to her and pulling Lyla into his arms. "We loved

Ann, but we love you, too. And we'll welcome you to this family with open arms."

Lyla still looked a little stunned but nowhere on the verge of saying yes.

"The tape?" Saul prompted again.

"Play it," Wyatt answered, but he took Lyla by the arm and marched her out into the hall.

She stared at him as if he'd lost him mind. Maybe he had, but he wasn't dropping this.

"What's on that tape could be important," Lyla said.

"Not more important than this."

She huffed. "You've made it clear. You want me to stay married to you. You want us to raise this baby—"

"I'm in love with you."

Like the earlier kiss, that stopped her. She stared at him, her expression softening. Well, it softened for a few seconds before she shook her head again.

"You haven't gotten over your wife's death," she added. "And until you do, you shouldn't be asking me or anyone else to marry you."

"I'll never get over that," he answered honestly. "She'll always be part of my life. But a part that I've put behind me so I can move on. With you and the baby."

She just stared at him.

"This would be a good time for you to realize you're in love with me," Wyatt tossed out there. He didn't expect much but hoped for the best.

Actually, he hoped for a miracle.

And he got one.

The corner of Lyla's mouth lifted. Barely a smile, and it didn't have time to grow into something bigger. That was because of the footsteps he heard heading right toward them.

Sheriff Geary was leading a handcuffed Zeke up the stairs and no doubt to a jail cell.

With her still in his arms, Wyatt ushered Lyla back into the room, where they got congrats and well-wishes, which were cut off when Zeke was brought in.

Zeke aimed glares at all of them, but that glare morphed to pure shock when he saw the tape recorder on the desk.

"Anything on there will be a lie," Zeke snarled.

As if to prove him wrong, Saul pressed the button on the recorder.

Just like that, the happy moment was gone, and they all seemed to hold their breaths. Even Billy.

"This is Sarah Webb," the voice said. And it was indeed Sarah, all right. "I'm making this tape because I believe my life's in danger. If something happens to me, then the person responsible is Sheriff Zeke Mercer."

There it was. Exactly what Wyatt had wanted to hear. But the tape wasn't over. She could still drag Kirby and the rest of them into this.

"Sheriff Zeke Mercer walked in on a fight between Jonah and me. We were in Stella's room because of a broken pipe, but Stella wasn't there. Jonah hit me, and in the heat of the argument, I grabbed his knife and stabbed him. Zeke's the one who pulled the knife out of his ribs."

That explained the castoff and why it didn't match a woman of Sarah's size.

"Jonah ran down the hall to his office and was going to get a gun and kill me," Sarah continued. Even though her voice was soft, it seemed to shout through the room. "I tried to wrestle the gun away from him, but he backhanded me. I fell, hit my head on the desk and lost consciousness. When I came to, Jonah was dead, his chest covered in blood, and Zeke helped me bury his body."

That was it, the end of the tape, and Wyatt mentally went through the explanation he'd just heard.

"The stab wound Sarah gave him didn't kill Webb, did it?" Wyatt asked Zeke.

Zeke just resumed his scowl.

"You killed him after Sarah was knocked out cold and then let her believe she'd done it."

Bingo. Wyatt saw the slight reaction in Zeke's eyes, letting him know he'd hit pay dirt.

"It doesn't matter if you don't confess," Kirby pressed. "You're already going down for Sarah's murder and for being an accessory. Plus, a whole boatload of other crimes that involve attempted murder of federal marshals. You'll get the death penalty whether you man up to this or not."

A muscle flickered in Zeke's jaw. "I'm more of a man than you'll ever be, Kirby Granger."

"Really?" Kirby challenged. "Then prove it. Man up."

The muscle flicked harder, and Zeke cursed some raw profanity. "Yeah, I did it. I killed Webb." And that was all he said for several long moments. Wyatt was worried his fit of temper had come and gone.

But it hadn't.

"Webb was blackmailing me for a business deal where he'd arranged to move those guns from Rocky Creek to Mexico, and he would have ruined me. That's why I went to see him that night, to try to reason with him, and I walked in on Sarah stabbing him."

"She didn't kill him," Billy mumbled.

"No. Barely made a cut, with the puny way she lunged at him with that knife. It only pissed him off, and he would have killed her if I hadn't stabbed him and finished the job."

Wyatt shook his head. "You didn't kill Webb to save Sarah. You did it because he was blackmailing you."

Zeke lifted his shoulder. "Doesn't matter none now, does it? It was easy killing him. And when Sarah came to and saw him dead, she just assumed she'd done it. I helped her bury the body."

"When did she tell you about the tape?" Lyla asked.

"A couple of days later. She said if anything happened to her, then everyone would learn that I'd been an accessory to murder."

None of them said anything, but Wyatt could feel the stunned silence. Zeke hadn't been just an accessory. He was the one who'd killed Webb.

"You nearly killed us, too," Lyla said, "when you had the bomb go off at Rocky Creek."

"That wasn't meant to kill you. If it had been, you'd be dead. It was to destroy that damn blood spatter that the CSI geeks found. I cut my hand when I pulled the knife from Webb, and I figured some of my blood could be mixed in with the castoff. I made an anonymous call to report the bomb so you could get out in time."

Wyatt had figured as much. At that point, Zeke would have still wanted Lyla alive so he could force her to manipulate any evidence that might incriminate him. That didn't mean, however, that they couldn't have died in that explosion.

"You're the one who had the embryo stolen," Wyatt said. He was certain of it, but he wanted the admission from the man who'd made their lives a living hell.

Zeke nodded, grumbled something under his breath. "You hadn't exactly kept it a secret that you wanted a kid, and, yeah, I figured you'd try to protect Lyla once she was pregnant. But I also figured you'd be so anxious to protect the baby she was carrying that you'd tell her to do whatever it took—and that included fixing any evidence against me."

It turned Wyatt's stomach to hear a fellow lawman accuse him of something like that. It was true that he would have protected Lyla and the baby, but Wyatt would have never forced her to tamper with evidence. He would have looked for another way. And had found it. That's why Zeke was under arrest right now.

"I'm bringing in your business partner, Greg," Saul informed Zeke.

"He did nothing wrong. Was just a kid when the killing happened, and he heard just enough not to have heard anything that would point to me. A lot of people had a beef with Webb that night."

"But you kept Greg close," Lyla said. "All these years you kept him by your side, in your business, in case he remembered the wrong thing."

"Maybe. But it doesn't matter now."

"It could," Lyla argued. "We got a call from an unknown name and number, It wasn't your voice, but it could have been Greg's. That would make him an accessory to your crimes."

"It wasn't Greg. I hired someone, a lackey, to make that call. I wouldn't have dragged Greg into this when it was easier to pay someone."

That was true, and it would have turned Greg into another loose end that Zeke might have to tie up.

Sheriff Geary started to lead Zeke toward the jail cell, but the man stopped directly in front of Kirby. "Jonah Webb got exactly what he deserved," Zeke snarled.

Kirby nodded. "Now you'll get what you deserve, too."

Zeke was still mumbling profanity when the sheriff hauled him away.

Despite the profanity and the somber mood, there was relief, too. And something else. The realization that for the first time in nearly seventeen years, there was no dark cloud hanging over his family.

But it was more than that.

Lyla was there. Part of it. And Wyatt pulled her back into his arms. "In the hall, I said this was a good time for you to realize you're in love with me."

"I'm in love with you," she whispered.

Now it was Wyatt's turn to lose his tongue. Yeah, it was exactly what he wanted her to say, but he sure as heck hadn't expected it.

"Say it again," he insisted. Because he had to make sure his ears weren't playing tricks on him.

"I'm in love with you," she repeated, and she kissed him.

Wyatt kissed her right back. In fact, he upped it a significant notch until they were breathless, giddy and probably stupid.

But it was the good kind of stupid.

"I want it all with you," he told her. "A family and home. I want you."

"And I want you," she answering, pulling him into another kiss.

That one, too, would have gone on a lot longer than planned if several of his brothers hadn't cleared their throats. Saul, too.

"That's the end of the tape," Saul said, giving them a flat look. "That means you lovebirds can head out and, well, celebrate or something."

Wyatt had the idea of hauling Lyla off to bed to celebrate. Apparently his brothers, Kirby and Stella had a similar thing in mind, because there was a lot of kissing going on in the room.

"Let's get out of here," Lyla said. "Take me home."

And this time there was no doubting what she meant. Wyatt scooped her up in his arms and headed *home*.

* * * * *

Look for more books,
including a brand-new miniseries,
from USA TODAY *bestselling author*
Delores Fossen later in 2014!
You can find them
wherever Harlequin Intrigue books are sold.

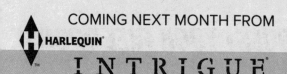

COMING NEXT MONTH FROM

HARLEQUIN®

INTRIGUE®

Available January 21, 2014

REQUEST YOUR FREE BOOKS!
2 FREE NOVELS PLUS 2 FREE GIFTS!

HARLEQUIN®

INTRIGUE®

BREATHTAKING ROMANTIC SUSPENSE

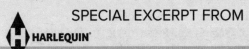
BLOOD ON COPPERHEAD TRAIL
by Paula Graves

Nothing can stop Laney Hanvey from looking for her missing sister. Not even sexy new chief of Bitterwood P.D....

"I'm not going to be handled out of looking for my sister," Laney growled as she heard footsteps catching up behind her on the hiking trail.

"I'm just here to help."

She faltered to a stop, turning to look at Doyle Massey. He wasn't exactly struggling to keep up with her—life on the beach had clearly kept him in pretty good shape. But he was out of his element.

She'd grown up in these mountains. Her mother had always joked she was half mountain goat, half Indian scout. She knew these hills as well as she knew her own soul. "You'll slow me down."

"Maybe that's a good thing."

She glared at him, her rising terror looking for a target. "My sister is out here somewhere and I'm going to find her."

The look Doyle gave her was full of pity. The urge to slap that expression off his face was so strong she had to clench her hands. "You're rushing off alone into the woods where a man with a gun has just committed a murder."

"A gun?" She couldn't stop her gaze from slanting toward the crime scene. "She was shot?"

"Two rounds to the back of the head."

She closed her eyes, the remains of the cucumber sandwich she'd eaten at Sequoyah House rising in her throat. She stumbled a few feet away from Doyle Massey and gave up fighting the nausea.

After her stomach was empty, she crouched in the underbrush, fighting dry heaves and giving in to the hot tears burning her eyes. The heat of Massey's hand on her back was comforting, even though she was embarrassed by her display.

"I will help you search," he said in a low, gentle tone. "But I want you to take a minute to just breathe and think. Okay? I want you to think about your sister and where you think she'd go. Do you know?"

Does Laney hold the key to her sister's whereabouts?
Doyle Massey intends to find out, in Paula Graves's
BLOOD ON COPPERHEAD TRAIL,
on sale in February 2014!